Hocus-Pocus
After School

by Candice F. Ransom

cover art by Gabriel
inside illustration by Estella Hickman

For Ryan, who let me "borrow"
his school projects

Published by Willowisp Press, Inc.
10100 SBF Drive, Pinellas Park, FL 34666

Copyright ©1992 by Willowisp Press, Inc.

Printed in the United States of America

2 4 6 8 10 9 7 5 3 1

ISBN 0-87406-591-7

One

TO tell you the truth, I never noticed anything weird about Mrs. Monicure until Lewis Butler came.

Up until then, I thought my after-school sitter was cool. Mrs. Monicure has two TV sets, one in the living room and one in the den, and she lets us kids watch whatever we want. She never nags us to do our homework. Plus she makes neat snacks. Little pizzas on English muffins, hot dogs stuffed with instant mashed potatoes, mustard-and-nothing sandwiches.

As I said, Mrs. Monicure was cool. But the very first day Lewis joined our group, he noticed something strange about her.

I'm jumping ahead of myself, as my mom is

forever telling me. "If you'd learn to concentrate, Cassandra," she'd say, "your grades would be better." She calls me Cassandra when she's mad.

She's wrong about my grades. They will never improve. I hate school. Well, not *school* exactly— I like recess and lunch and assemblies. I just hate the work they make you do in school. There's so *much* of it—board work, seat work, homework. Too much for any ten-year-old, I complained to my parents at the beginning of fifth grade. I didn't get much sympathy.

"School is easy," my dad said. "Your school days are the best days of your life."

Maybe school was easy for my parents, but it's hard for me. My parents are both smart, and they can't understand how they wound up with a dummy for a kid. My mother has a job at an insurance company. She adjusts claims. My father teaches physics at Walt Whitman High School. Physics is a kind of science. Dad believes there is a law for every single thing that happens in the universe. Nothing is an accident. One time when I dropped a carton of orange juice, I tried to blame it on the law of gravity. But I still had to clean it up.

It's pretty hard to get away with anything in my house. That's one reason I love going to Mrs. Monicure's after school. Mrs. Monicure lets "her kids," as she calls us, do anything we want, as long as we don't leave her property (something to do with insurance) and nobody gets hurt. That includes hurt feelings.

I've been going to Mrs. Monicure's house after school for three years, ever since Mom decided to go back to work. I was only in third grade then, too young to stay home by myself. So Mom found Mrs. Monicure to watch me after school until she got off work.

Mom picks me up on her way home from the insurance office. I don't mind if she's late sometimes because Mrs. Monicure will fix a special treat like beanie weenies for me and Oliver. Oliver's mother never comes before 6:30 or 7:00.

Oliver and Mrs. Monicure are sort of like a second family to me. Mrs. Monicure is like the grandmothers you read about in books, always puttering around in the garden or the kitchen. My real grandmother lives in California and runs in marathons. Oliver is like the brother I don't have. He looks up to me. Oliver thought I was the greatest—that is, until Lewis came.

I first noticed Lewis on the playground at school. Both fifth-grade classes were playing volleyball, our room against Mrs. Griffin's room. A big sandy-haired kid I'd never seen before stepped up to serve the ball for the other team.

"Who's he?" I asked Melanie, who was standing next to me.

Melanie shrugged. "Some new kid. I saw him in the office this morning when I took down the lunch slips." It seemed awfully late in the year to be transferred to a new school. We only had eight more weeks of school left.

Silence fell over the volleyball court as everyone turned to stare at the new kid. He clutched the volleyball in his hands as if he wanted to squeeze the air out of it. He stood a head taller than any other kid in Mrs. Griffin's class. Finally he got into position to serve the ball. Big as he was, I expected him to smash a real killer serve.

But the new kid barely tapped the ball. It didn't even clear the second row of his own team!

"Wimp! Wimp!" jeered the loud-mouthed Bradley Dunsbury, who was serving next for us. "What a pathetic hit!"

Normally, I would have yelled at Bradley for making fun of somebody, but he was on my team, and his next serve went right between two players. Our point!

When the other team got the serve back, the sandy-haired kid didn't know enough to move as his team rotated. When the new server practically pushed him out of the way, the boy ran off the field. Mrs. Griffin hurried after him.

I forgot all about the new kid until it was time to go home. As I climbed on the bus, ready to plop into my regular seat behind the bus driver, I stopped.

The sandy-haired kid was sitting in *my* seat. Nobody ever sat in my seat. I wasn't about to give it up, not to a wimpy, new kid.

"You're in my seat," I told Lewis, giving him my

very nastiest stare.

He glanced up at me. "Take a picture, it lasts longer," he said.

I turned red, which made me even madder. But he stared right back. "You're in my seat," I said again.

"I don't see your name on it."

"Everybody knows it's my seat. Get out!"

"Who's going to make me?"

"Me."

"Whoa, I'm shaking," he said with a smile.

I hesitated. He might have been a wimpy volleyball server, but he was still a lot bigger than I was. By now, there was a line of grumbling kids behind me. Mrs. Phillips, the driver, came to the front of the bus. "What's going on?" she asked. "Sandra, sit down. You're blocking the aisle."

"I can't. This kid is in my seat."

"I was here first," the new boy said.

Mrs. Phillips slid behind the wheel and said, "There's room for both of you. Lewis, move over."

He stood up. "I'm not sitting beside a girl. Especially not this girl! I'd rather sit on the floor."

"Don't bother, Lewissssss!" I said. "I'll find another seat—in the back of the bus!"

I stomped down the aisle and found an empty seat over the wheel. Putting my feet up on the tire hump, I rehearsed the story that I'd tell Mrs. Monicure as soon as I got to her house. She'd cluck her tongue and agree with me that Lewis what's-his-name was a jerk. Then she'd give me a hug and an extra treat—maybe a chocolate chip cookie warmed in the oven.

The bus eased up to the curb of Mrs. Monicure's corner. I hopped off and then turned to wave to Mrs. Phillips. It wasn't her fault that new Lewis kid stole my seat. But I noticed that somebody else was getting off at my stop.

Lewis clumped along behind me.

I stopped. "Where are you going?"

"None of your business," he muttered. He looked at a grubby scrap of paper and then checked the mailboxes lining the street.

All of a sudden I had a horrible feeling, like you get in an elevator when your stomach feels like it's falling out. "You're not going to 9109, are

10

you?" I asked. That was Mrs. Monicure's house.

"What's it to you if I am?"

"Well, you'd better not," I said, my stomach still sinking.

He followed me up Mrs. Monicure's sidewalk and stood on the porch while I waited for Mrs. Monicure to let me in. She'd tell him to get off her property in a hurry. Maybe she'd even threaten to call the police.

Mrs. Monicure opened the door wide and said, smiling, "Hello, Sandra. How are you today? I see you've met the newest member of our little group."

"*He's* coming here now?" I asked bluntly.

"Yes, he is. Lewis, come in and make yourself at home."

It was true. Lewis, the wimpy volleyball server and seat-stealer, was now in my group.

"Oliver, I'd like you to meet Lewis Butler," Mrs. Monicure said to Oliver, who was watching a nature program on TV. "He'll be staying with us from now on. Lewis, this is Oliver Cantrell. Now that you've met everybody in our little group, you can put your things on that chair by the door."

Lewis dropped his knapsack with a clunk on the floor. He glared at Mrs. Monicure.

But she just nodded. "I'll go fix you and Sandra something to eat."

I figured Lewis was testing Mrs. Monicure by throwing his stuff on the floor. He'd find out soon that Mrs. Monicure wasn't like other grown-ups. She didn't make a big deal of things.

Oliver bounced over to me. "Guess what we have today, Sandra? Strawberry shortcakes. Mrs. M. let me have extra Cool Whip."

"So what, shorty?" Lewis muttered.

"Just ignore him," I said to Oliver.

With a sidelong glance at Lewis, Oliver showed me his latest nature find. "See my new specimen? I found it out in the garden. Isn't it neat?" He held up his bug bottle so that I could see the hairy spider crawling up a leaf.

"A spider," I said with a shiver.

"It's a furrow spider," he said, pushing his glasses up on his nose. His glasses were always sliding down his nose. Oliver was a fourth-grader at a private school, but he never acted snooty. Mrs. Monicure said Oliver felt things more than most people. She told me this after Oliver's father died last year. Myself, I wasn't wild about spiders, but Oliver loved anything to do with nature.

Suddenly, Lewis grabbed the bug bottle out of Oliver's hand. "Let me see," he demanded. He shook the jar, making the furrow spider flop all over the place.

"Don't!" Oliver shrieked. "You'll hurt him!"

"Aww, don't bawl. It's just a dumb spider," Lewis said, shoving the bottle back at Oliver.

Mrs. Monicure came in with two dishes of strawberry shortcake. She'd split two cakes, covered them with fresh strawberries and topped the whole creation with whipped cream.

"Here you go, Sandra. Lewis, if you want seconds, just holler. I'll be in the kitchen if you need anything." Mrs. Monicure pretty much left us kids alone, unless we had a problem. Last year, after Oliver's father died, she spent a lot of time with Oliver.

I sat down at the far end of the sofa and began

eating. Lewis sat next to me. Oliver went back to his TV show. Aiming his spoon like a slingshot, Lewis fired a gob of Cool Whip. It landed on the back of Oliver's head.

"Quit it," I warned.

Lewis laughed. "He doesn't know it's there."

"I do too," Oliver said quietly.

"Why are you here?" I demanded.

"Believe me, it wasn't *my* idea." Lewis scraped his dish clean and plunked it on the coffee table. "What a stupid house. Isn't there anything to do around here? At home I have 27 video games."

I choked on a strawberry. Twenty-seven video games! Lewis Butler must be rich.

"Hey, you and me could be against Sandra," Lewis said, suddenly buddy-buddy to Oliver.

"I don't want to be against Sandra," Oliver answered him.

"Eh, you're too little anyway." Lewis looked over at me. "Maybe you and I should gang up against the little kid. We're the oldest. We should be running the show," he said.

I set him straight. "Nobody runs the show

around here. We're all equals."

"You mean you and Four Eyes do the same things?" Lewis hooted. "Sandra's play group. Hey! I think we should have a club!"

Oliver looked up. He was interested, even though Lewis called him Four Eyes. "What kind of a club?"

"A club just for us after-school kids," Lewis replied. "We'll do all kinds of neat stuff. I'll be the president."

"Why you?" I asked.

"Because I'm the biggest." Nobody could argue with that.

"Well, nobody cares how big you are," I said. "Come on, Oliver, let's go outside."

But Oliver hung back. "What would we do in the club, Lewis?" he asked.

A club! Darn it! Why hadn't I ever thought of that? Oliver liked the games I made up. *I* was the leader at Mrs. Monicure's. But not any longer, I realized, as I took my dish into the kitchen.

Mrs. Monicure was mixing something in a bowl. "What's wrong, Sandra?" she asked.

"It's that new kid."

"Lewis?"

"He's terrible."

She smiled. "He's just a little unsure of himself right now. You'll get used to him."

"I'll *never* get used to him. I don't like him!"

"Now, Sandra, give him a chance. Where did I put that salt?" Mrs. M. asked.

Out of the corner of my eye, I saw Lewis standing in the doorway. He must have heard what I said. I didn't care. I meant every word.

He stomped into the kitchen and slammed his dish on the counter. As he passed me, he stepped hard on my foot.

"Oh, excuse me," he said sarcastically.

"You did that on purpose!" I whispered.

Mrs. Monicure was looking through the cupboards. "Where is that salt?" she asked.

Just then, her cat Shadow leaped up on the counter. His eyes were yellow slits in his midnight fur. "Mur-row," said the cat rubbing against Mrs. M.'s arm.

"You're right, Shadow," Mrs. Monicure muttered. "I have to show that snippety salt who's boss in this kitchen. Salt!" she commanded. Then she sort of waved her hand, and the salt shaker was next to the mixing bowl.

"Took your sweet time, didn't you?" Mrs. M. said. She couldn't have been talking to the salt shaker, could she? But she sure wasn't talking to me or Lewis.

Lewis's eyes widened. He grabbed my arm and pulled me into the dining room.

"Did you see what she did? With the salt?"

I yanked my arm away. "Of course I saw. I'm not blind."

"First she knew what the cat said. Then she called the salt! It wasn't there and then it was!"

"It was there all the time," I answered. "She just didn't see it."

"No way!" Lewis said. "She *called* it and it appeared. Like magic!"

I rubbed my arm where he had squeezed it. "What are you babbling about?"

"Sandra," Lewis said, breathless with excitement, "our babysitter is a witch!"

Two

"A witch?" a voice echoed.

I whirled around. Oliver stood there with his spider jar, his blue eyes were round as dinner plates.

"Did he say Mrs. M. is a witch?" Oliver asked.

"Don't listen to Lewis," I said. "He's nuts."

"I'm not nuts!" Lewis said. "She *is* a witch!"

I put my hands on my hips. "If Mrs. M.'s a witch, how come we haven't noticed before? I've been here a lot longer than you have. So has Oliver."

Lewis shrugged. "Can I help it if you're not very observant? Or maybe...maybe the old lady put a spell on you guys so that you wouldn't notice."

"How come she didn't put a spell on you?" Oliver pointed out in his logical way.

"Yeah! Can you answer that one, Lewis?"

Lewis rolled his eyes as if he were dealing with idiots. "You guys are so dumb. That's what she was doing in the kitchen! Mixing up my spell! Only she couldn't find the salt, and then we came in and she had to stop. She couldn't stir up my spell while we were standing there, could she?"

I burst out laughing. "Talk about being dumb! Mrs. Monicure was mixing up biscuits!"

"Did she *say* she was mixing up biscuits?" Lewis asked.

"Well, no, but anybody with half a brain—"

"Yeah, like you," Lewis said. Then he shifted his sly gaze to Oliver. "Hey, kid, is there a basketball hoop or anything around this place?"

"No, but we can throw a ball in the driveway. If you want," Oliver added. It sounded as if he still wasn't sure of Lewis.

Lewis smacked him on the shoulder in a big-brother way. "Sounds great. Let's make like the wind and blow."

"I'm going to play with Lewis," Oliver said. "Will you watch my jar, Sandra?" Thrusting the spider jar into my hands, he ran outside.

I stood in the dining room, fuming. First Lewis insults me and Oliver and then he accuses Mrs. M. of being a witch, and now all of a sudden he's acting buddy-buddy to Oliver. There was a lot I didn't like about Lewis Butler.

The spider scuttled up the slick sides of the jar, only to slide down again. He climbed up again and again. I was sorry for him. I knew how it felt to be trapped. I felt that way in school all the time. And I was beginning to feel that way about being at Mrs. M.'s with that awful Lewis.

I went out the front door. At the bottom of the steps, I opened the jar and shook the spider out. Setting the spider free made me feel better, though I'd have to confess to Oliver that I let his specimen go.

Walking around back, I found Lewis and Oliver crouched in Mrs. M.'s garden. They weren't playing catch at all. I saw that Oliver's eyes were round as I crept closer to hear what Lewis was telling him.

"—does her flying when nobody's around. I bet the broomstick comes when she calls it, too."

"Stop it!" I yelled. Lewis was scaring Oliver half to death.

Lewis whipped around. "You shouldn't sneak up on people like that!"

"And *you* shouldn't tell wild stories!" I said.

"Lewis says Mrs. M. is a witch," Oliver said. "Is she, Sandra? Is Mrs. Monicure really a witch?"

A car pulled up to the curb out front. "Is that your mother, Oliver? She's early," I said. "You'd better get your stuff."

He jumped up. "Oh, boy! Maybe we're going to Burger Biz. See you tomorrow, Sandra. Later, Lewis."

"Later, dude."

Later. What kind of talk was Lewis teaching Oliver?

"Listen," I said to Lewis after Oliver had left. "You shouldn't fill Oliver's head with that witch stuff. He's very—" *What was the word my mother used?* "—impressionable. Especially now."

21

I told Lewis how Oliver's father had died last year. Mr. Cantrell had been sick a long time, as long as Oliver and I had been staying at Mrs. Monicure's after school. Oliver missed his father a lot. He hung around me more and more. I liked having Oliver look up to me. He was the little brother I didn't have, and I was the older sister he didn't have. Only children had to stick together.

And now Lewis was ruining everything. Oliver wanted to spend time with him instead of me.

"You're jealous," Lewis jeered.

"I am not!"

"You're jealous because the shrimp likes me."

"He doesn't like you," I said angrily. "He's only hanging around you to hear about this stupid witch stuff."

"It's not stuff. It's true. The old lady is definitely a witch," Lewis answered, pulling the petals off a tulip. His smile made me mad. "Just because you don't believe me—"

He was such a fake. He made up the witch story, just to make himself look cool. Then suddenly, it came to me how I could put Lewis in his place.

"Prove it," I said. "If you can show me Mrs. M. is really and truly a witch, I'll believe you. And I'll even say it in front of Oliver, that you were right and I was wrong."

He grinned slowly, like a crocodile. "You're on! We'll start tomorrow after school."

"Huh-uh. We'll start sooner than that," I said. "Let's meet in the school library before class tomorrow morning. Meet me at the table under the clock."

* * * * *

There weren't many books about witches in our school library. In fact, there was only one, a tired-looking book called *Witchcraft Through the Ages*. Maybe the teachers were afraid we'd cook up a spell to get out of doing homework or pass tests without studying.

Lewis and I took the book over to a corner table and opened it. "Mrs. M. doesn't look like that," I said, stabbing my finger at a drawing of an old crone in an ugly, black dress.

"Of course not," Lewis answered. "This is the 20th century. She'd stick out like a sore thumb if she went around in that get-up."

The stuff Lewis read, while I took notes, was kind of neat. The word *witch* comes from *wicca*, which means "wise one" in some old language. Witches knew a lot about making medicines from plants, before pills were invented. They could cure warts and mix up love potions. Lewis made a face at that part, but I wrote it down anyway.

Next we read how witches put hexes on their enemies to get rid of them. "Gee, I wish they had that spell in here," Lewis said, flipping through the book. "That could come in handy."

"It sure could," I said.

We read about how regular people like us could protect ourselves against witches by carrying metal. Nuts and apples are protection, too— I guess witches don't like wholesome foods.

"Think," Lewis said. "Does Mrs. M. ever have apples in her house?"

"Everybody has apples," I said. But actually,

I couldn't ever remember seeing apples in the fruit bowl Mrs. M. kept on top of her refrigerator.

Suddenly Lewis said, "This is it. Here's what we're looking for. Witch's powers!"

I wrote fast. When he finished reading, my notes looked like this:

Witching hour—midnight on a full moon. Witch's powers increase and decrease with the moon. Powers lowest during dark of moon, highest in full moon. Carry charms. Have a book of spells called a "grimoire."

Neither of us could pronounce that last word, but we figured out what it meant. "This is what we need to find," he said. "We have to find Mrs. M.'s book of spells. Then we'll know for sure she's a witch."

*　*　*　*　*

"I don't like this, Lewis." I hesitated in the doorway of Mrs. Monicure's bedroom. "We shouldn't snoop through other people's things."

Lewis pushed past me. "It's the only way,

Sandra. How else will we get evidence that old lady M. is a witch?"

"She's *not* an old lady," I answered, glancing nervously out the window over Mrs. Monicure's bed. I could see her on her knees digging in the garden. Oliver was with her, yakking a mile a minute. He was supposed to keep her occupied while we searched her bedroom.

"Well, she's not young either," Lewis said. "See if she's got any black dresses. I'll look for the book of spells." He slid open a bureau drawer and began rifling through scarves and gloves.

Mrs. Monicure's bedroom looked about as witchy as an Easter egg. Pink ruffled curtains puffed at the windows. A pink and blue quilt covered the bed, and a mountain of yellow and pink pillows were piled at one end. There were green, fluffy rugs on the floor, and the dresser was crammed with perfume bottles.

"The closet!" Lewis reminded me. I opened the closet. Inside, hanging neatly from the pole, were flowered tops and slacks in every color of the rainbow. There were shoes on the floor. Pocketbooks dangled from a strap. A few dresses hung in the back, but none of them were black.

The back door slammed. Lewis and I stared at each other for a heart-stopping second, and then he quickly tossed scarves and stockings back in the drawer. I shut the closet, hoping nothing was out of order.

We got out just in time. Mrs. Monicure was coming down the hall, her hands grimy with dirt.

"You ought to be out in the sunshine," she said. "Enjoy this lovely spring day."

"Uh, we're going outside in a minute," I said.

"That was close," Lewis whispered as Mrs. M. went into the bathroom.

"It was stupid! We didn't find a thing, which proves you're dead wrong!" I hissed. I couldn't wait to tell the truth to Oliver, that Mrs. Monicure was just a nice lady who liked pink curtains and growing flowers.

After Mrs. M. went back outside, Lewis raided the pantry. "What are you hunting for now?" I demanded.

"A broom." His voice was muffled. "The broom

she rides on when the moon is full. It'll probably tingle when we touch it, it'll be so loaded with magic." He paused. "All I see is this."

He pulled out a skinny, vacuum-cleaner type of gadget. Very unmagical looking.

"That's her electric broom," I said. I just shook my head.

Lewis tugged at the cord. "An *electric* broom? How can she ride this thing?" He picked up a little plug-in hand vacuum. "Maybe the cat rides this little one," Lewis added.

I snickered. "Right! Can you see Shadow flying through the air on a mini electric broom! And Mrs. M. on her electric broom!"

Lewis shoved the vacuum back in the pantry. "Very funny. You'll sing a different tune when we find that book of spells."

There was only one logical place to search for the book of spells, the *grimoire*. Lewis sat on the rug and began pulling books from the bookcase.

"Mushy stuff," he muttered. "Yuck!"

I stacked the books and put them back in the bookcase. They were all paperback romance

books, with pink or purple covers showing ladies bent backward over the arms of handsome men. Mrs. M. bought a new book at the grocery store every week, along with one of those newspapers that always had Elvis or UFOs or both in the headlines.

When Lewis was through pitching books, he looked disappointed. "All right," I said. "What kind of a witch has an electric broom, wears flowered blouses, and reads romance novels? Give up?"

Lewis didn't say anything.

I went on. "Mrs. M doesn't have a black dress *or* a book of spells *or* even a broom. So what kind of a witch *is* she, Lewis?"

Now he would have to admit he was wrong. I'd make him say it again in front of Oliver. Then Oliver would realize what I knew all along, that Lewis Butler was a loudmouthed jerk.

He ran his hand through his hair, obviously trying to think his way out of this one.

"She's, uh—" Then his face lit up. "She's an everyday witch! That's it! Mrs. Monicure is an everyday witch. She probably practices ordinary magic, like calling the salt and stuff. I bet she was demoted by the head witch, and that's why we can't find her book of spells."

I groaned. "Oh, man. You are too weird." I went outside to find Oliver. He was playing with a toad he had found.

"Isn't he neat? Mrs. Monicure says it's lucky to have a toad in the garden." He prodded the toad with his finger to make him hop for me.

Although it was only mid-April, Mrs. M.'s garden was in full bloom. There were tulips and lilies and other flowers I didn't know the names of, plus a million little green plants Oliver said were herbs. The neighbors had gardens, too, but theirs were still brown from the winter. Only a few plants had started to show pale green leaves. I wondered why Mrs. M.'s garden seemed so far ahead of everyone else's.

"Why is it so green here?" I murmured.

"Because she does stuff to it," said Oliver. I guessed that he meant she put fertilizer and manure on her plants.

"She's not a witch, you know," I told him. "Lewis and I looked for her broom and a black dress and the book of spells. We couldn't find a thing. Lewis was just making it all up."

Oliver didn't seem to care. "I like Lewis," he said. "I think he's neat."

"He's not neat. He's a troublemaker. You shouldn't believe what he says."

Just then, the troublemaker himself came huffing up. For a big kid, Lewis wasn't in very good shape. "She just went in the house," he reported. "Let's go spy on her. I bet she does something witchy."

Oliver leaped up, his toad and my speech forgotten. "Okay!" he cried.

"Wait, you guys," I called, but there was no stopping them. I ran to catch up. Lewis and Oliver crouched in the bushes under the window and peered into the living room. Because it was such a warm day, Mrs. M. had the window open. I felt awful spying on my own babysitter. We watched as she came into the room with her latest newspaper. She sat in the chair across from the TV, put her feet up on the coffee table, opened the paper and started to read.

Then she frowned. The corner she was sitting in was kind of dark. "Light," she said. Nothing happened. "Light," she said again, impatiently. The lamp flickered, then stayed on.

Lewis pulled us away from the window. "Did you see that?"

"She made the light come on," Oliver said, awestruck.

"She did not!" I argued. "She probably just got one of those things you plug in and your voice turns on the lamp and TV. My aunt has one. All she does is clap and the light goes off."

But nobody was listening to me. I could tell Oliver would rather believe that Mrs. Monicure ordered the lamp to turn itself on. He *wanted* to believe she was a witch. Lewis already believed she was a witch. I was the only one who didn't.

And I was losing ground, fast.

Three

LEWIS BUTLER IS A BIG FAT DU—

I was searching for the "m" key on the school computer when Mr. Crowley came up behind me.

"Cassandra," he said, scaring me so that I hit the "delete" key by mistake. Now my sentence read *Lewis Butler is a big fat d.* "Is this your book project?" my teacher asked.

"Well, uhh ..." If only I had hit the key to wipe out the whole sentence instead of one letter.

"I thought so." He leaned over my computer terminal to deliver his daily lecture. "Cassandra," he said. He always called me by my real name. "You know the write-a-book project is due at the end of the year. That's only a few short weeks away. The others are working on their final

34

drafts. I haven't seen your outline yet. When do you plan to start this project?"

"Uhh, today," I fibbed.

His eyebrow lifted. He'd heard that one before. "How about right now?" he asked.

"Right this second? As soon as I think of an idea," I answered. "It's hard to think up an idea just like that."

Mr. Crowley sighed, making the little hairs of his mustache blow out. "Cassandra, you've had since the first of the year to begin this project. You were supposed to submit a list of ideas so that I could help you choose the best one."

I scrabbled through a pile of notebook papers beside the computer. "I have a list here somewhere. Well, part of a list, anyway. Nope, not here. Must have left it at home."

With another sigh, Mr. Crowley said, "See me after class, Cassandra."

I knew what that meant. Note time. Mr. Crowley was going to write another note home to my parents. This note would join the others in the bottom drawer of my dresser. Of course, Mr.

Crowley was no fool. If he didn't get an answer within a week, he'd call my mother and tell her I wasn't doing my projects, and then *she'd* get on my case.

But that wouldn't happen for at least a week.

After writing lab, I took the sealed envelope Mr. Crowley gave me and put it in my backpack. I complained to Melanie at lunch.

"Teachers give us too much work for the end of the year," I grumbled, tearing my cheese sandwich into bite-sized pieces. "They must think we're slaves or something."

"We only have two projects," Melanie pointed out. "The book and the skeleton. I'm almost finished with my book."

She didn't ask if mine was nearly finished because she knew I hadn't even started. "The skeleton is even harder," I said. "Imagine making us draw a whole human skeleton! All those bones! There must be a million!"

"Actually, 206," Melanie said. "I finished it last week. I would have been done sooner, but I had to copy it twice. Have you done yours, Sandra?

It counts as one-third of our science grade."

"I know," I answered.

"I heard Mr. Crowley getting after you today," she said. "You really *should* start the book project, Sandra. You're the only one in class who hasn't. It counts as half our English grade."

"I don't care if it's worth our whole grade," I said. "It's not fair teachers make us do creative stuff. I can't think of an idea. I've tried!"

Melanie looked at me over her milk carton. "Not even *one* idea?"

"Not even a crummy *part* of an idea. I just can't think up stuff like that."

Everyday school work was bad enough, but projects were the worst. Teachers were forever dreaming up some awful thing for us to do, something to keep us awake at night, worrying over how to do it.

"That kid's looking at you," Melanie said suddenly.

"What kid?"

Across the lunchroom, Lewis was sitting by himself. His class ate lunch the same time mine did. Lewis came to our school too late in the year to make any friends. Not that he'd *ever* have a friend, even if he had started fifth grade the second he was born.

When he saw me looking at him, he grinned around the nacho he had in his mouth. Cheese dripped down his chin. He raised his hands to his ears and clenched them like witch's claws.

"Gross." Melanie wrinkled her nose. "What a nerd."

"He's the nerd to end all nerds," I pronounced.

Watching Lewis made me lose what was left of my appetite. Could life get any worse? I had two school projects looming over my head, and when school was out, I had to deal with Lewis Butler, the cheese-slobbering, fifth-grade witch hunter.

* * * * *

As I passed Lewis on the bus, I fell over his big, cloddy feet which were sticking out in the aisle.

"Do you have to trip me every single day?" I asked. "Don't you ever give it a rest?"

"Sorry," he said, with that maddening grin. "I didn't mean to, Sandra. I don't want to get my posterboard dirty."

I noticed the white sheets angled against his seat. Okay, so he had a legitimate excuse this time, but what about every other day? He didn't ask me to sit with him. Not that I would. I found my seat over the tire and sat by myself, staring glumly at the passing trees and houses.

At our stop, Lewis hopped off the bus ahead of me, carrying his sheets of posterboard like a kite. "I bought this stuff today in the supply store," he said, as if I cared. "I have to draw a skeleton."

"Do you have to write a book, too?"

He shook his head as we walked up to Mrs. Monicure's front porch. "I came too late. But I have to write a story on the computer. We didn't have a computer at my old school. It's neat."

I had never asked Lewis where he went before he came to Oak View Elementary. All I knew was that he was a real pest.

Oliver opened the door for us. "We're making

39

pie-dough roll-ups!" he said excitedly.

"Blecchh," Lewis said. "Sounds awful. I don't want any."

I put my backpack on the chair. "Good. I'll eat yours." Mrs. M.'s pie-dough roll-ups were great.

Lewis changed his mind when he got a whiff of cinnamon and butter. We went into the kitchen, where Mrs. Monicure was rolling out dough. She cut out circles of dough, sprinkled them with cinnamon and sugar, and then rolled them into cigar shapes. Oliver lined the cigar shapes on the baking sheet.

"My mother used to make these out of dough scraps whenever she made a pie," Mrs. M. said. "I always liked the roll-ups better than the pie!" Mrs. Monicure laughed. "I told myself when I grew up, I'd make all roll-ups instead of baking a pie."

Lewis smirked at me. "Can you see her as a little witch?" he said under his breath.

I jabbed his ribs. "Be quiet! She'll hear."

But Mrs. Monicure didn't seem to hear anything. She slid the pan into the oven, and then poured us each a big glass of milk. "The roll-ups will be done in a minute. What's that you've got there, Lewis?" she asked.

He spread his posterboard on the kitchen table. "I have to draw a skeleton for science."

"All those bones? My, that's a tall assignment for a child," Mrs. M. said.

"I have to draw one, too," I said. Usually I never mentioned I had any homework, but I didn't want Mrs. Monicure to think Lewis was the only one with tough assignments.

"Let's do it now," he said suddenly. "Together. You can borrow some of my posterboard."

The last thing I wanted to do was draw that awful skeleton, but Lewis was already setting out marker pens and pencils. He told Oliver to turn to page 111 in his science book. A full-length skeleton covered the page. We were supposed to copy it and label the bones.

"Come on," Lewis urged. "It won't take long."

"You children do your homework," Mrs. M. said. "Oliver and I will stay out of your way."

I have to admit, it was kind of neat doing a

school project in Mrs. M.'s kitchen. Lewis even seemed nice when he was busy working. I started to think maybe he wasn't quite so bad after all. Shadow came in and perched on the windowsill. He washed his paws, eyeing our nice clean posterboard now and then, as if he wanted to mess it up. The roll-ups smelled yummy and tasted even yummier when Oliver brought a plate of the first batch to us. Lewis gobbled them down faster than I did.

The phone rang. Mrs. Monicure went into the living room to answer it. It must have been an old friend because she talked a long time.

"We're never going to finish this today," I said, sketching a lopsided skull in black marker.

"I am," Lewis declared. "I'll show you." He took a sheet of tracing paper from his notebook and laid it over the picture of the skeleton in the book. He began tracing the drawing.

"Hey! No fair!" I yelled. "That's cheating. We're supposed to draw it freehand."

"Can I help it my hand is a little freer than when most kids draw?"

Oliver, who had been leafing through Mrs. M.'s cookbook, came over to see what we were arguing about. He studied our drawings.

"Lewis's is a lot better than yours," he said.

"Because he traced it!" I yelled. "I ought to tell his teacher."

Lewis put the final touches on his skeleton. It looked terrific. "She won't believe you. Nobody can tell I traced it. See, I messed up this part so that it doesn't look so good."

Mrs. Monicure came back in and surveyed our work. "Very nice, Lewis," she said. To me she said, "Sandra, I think you're going to run out of room. You should have started in the middle of the paper."

I had drawn my skull along the left edge of my posterboard. Now that I was drawing the collarbone, I realized I wouldn't have room for the arms, unless I squished them along the rib cage.

"I have enough room," I said stubbornly. "My picture will look just as good as his." But inside, I was steaming.

At home that evening, I finished my skeleton

44

drawing. I was labeling the bones in teeny-tiny printing (because there wasn't any room), when my father walked past the table.

"Sandra," he said, "is that your science project?" I nodded, printing *femur* in letters so small that it hurt my eyes to write them. "Why did you cram your drawing in the corner like that? You know that won't be acceptable to Mr. Crowley."

"Yes, it will." Mr. Crowley would probably faint if I actually turn something in on time.

"No, it won't," he answered. "I'm a science teacher, and I know I wouldn't give that project a passing grade. Your mother told me the skeleton is one-third of your final grade in science."

Hmm. I guess Mr. Crowley didn't wait a whole week to call my mother. I'd been hiding the notes from my teacher for nothing.

"Sandra, you'll have to do it over," Dad said.

"But it took me hours to do this!" I wailed.

Dad took out a clean piece of posterboard and made a tiny mark in the center. "Start the top of your skull there. Then you'll have enough room."

I worked on my skeleton until 10:30. When

Mom announced my bedtime at 9:30, I told her Dad was making me do my science project over. I hoped she'd feel sorry for me, but she left me alone. My second skeleton drawing wasn't so hot, either, but at least it wasn't all crowded and you could read the labels without going blind.

The next day, Mr. Crowley graded the drawings. My skeleton looked pretty pitiful pinned on the wall with the others. But Mr. Crowley seemed happy that I actually turned in a project. He gave me a C.

"What'd you get?" I asked Lewis on the bus going to Mrs. Monicure's house. He proudly pulled out his traced skeleton. A big red A and a smiley face decorated one corner of his posterboard. I wanted to wipe that grin off his face.

My parents were always nagging me to do my best work. Maybe my best wasn't so hot most of the time, but at least I didn't cheat.

"We're not playing with Lewis today," I said to Oliver as soon as I walked in the door. Mrs. Monicure was in her garden. I could see her from the window. She didn't like it when we kids didn't play together. Oliver didn't even hear me. He ran straight over to Lewis. "Lewis!" he cried. "I found it!"

"Found what, kid?"

Oliver was so excited that he couldn't stop hopping up and down. "The book! The witch book you guys were looking for!"

Four

"THE book of spells? You found the book of spells?" Lewis asked.

"I think so." Behind his thick glasses, Oliver's eyes were round and serious.

Lewis smacked him on the back so hard that he nearly fell over. "Way to go, kid! Where is it?"

Oliver straightened up, grinning. I think he loved it when Lewis acted buddy-buddy, even if it half-killed him. "It's in the kitchen," he said. "Come on, Sandra!"

I had decided to wash my hands of this witch business. It was all in Lewis's head. But curiosity made me follow the boys into the kitchen. Mrs. Monicure's cookbook lay open on the table.

"That's it," Oliver said proudly.

"That?" Lewis flashed me a doubtful glance. "It's just an old cookbook," Lewis said, flipping through the pages. "I don't see any spells," he added with disgust. "Just a bunch of recipes."

"In the back," Oliver whispered, turning over the last divider. "The section called Special Hints."

The sheets in the very back of the cookbook weren't like the other pages. These were yellowed notebook pages, not fastened in. The writing on them was old-fashioned and faint, written in soft pencil. I picked up one of the sheets.

"How to Sour Milk," I read.

Lewis grabbed the other sheets and read the titles. "How to Keep a Cake from Falling, How to Cure Warts."

I couldn't keep the smirk off my face. "Pretty pathetic spells, if you ask me. Where are the powerful ones we read about? Like how to make people disappear?"

Lewis pawed through the rest of the yellowed sheets, but the "spells" were just as boring.

"Make Your Own Bluing Soap from Ashes and Lye, How to Preserve the Perfume of Wildflowers.

What is this stuff?" he asked.

"I think they're old-timey household tips," I said. "You know, like that column in the newspaper, 'Tips from Debbie.'"

"Not magic spells?" Oliver looked disappointed. I think he wanted Mrs. Monicure to be a witch almost as much as Lewis did.

"Enough is enough, Lewis! Give up on this stupid witch stuff!" I cried.

Lewis's eyebrows drew together as his gray eyes darkened. "You wouldn't believe the old lady was a witch if she rode her broom right in front of you. If you're so smart, Cassandra Higgins, how come you get such lousy grades in school?"

With a scream, I stomped out of the kitchen, banging the back door. I wandered into Mrs. Monicure's garden. She had finished setting out new plants and was trimming the hedge on the far side of the yard. I waved and some of my anger went away. Mrs. M. was the greatest person in the world. She was the only person who wasn't on my case about something.

Lewis came out, munching an oatmeal cookie.

Oliver scuffled along behind him.

"Sorry, you guys," Oliver said. "I thought that book was what you were hunting for."

"Forget it, kid." Lewis sat down in the warm dirt. "She probably hid her book of spells someplace really hard to find. Nothing is ever easy."

"How would you know?" I said. "You cheat on your homework—that's easy, if you ask me."

"Nobody asked you." He squinted in the sun. "I hate this town. I wish I were back in Maryland."

"So do I."

Oops. As soon as the words left my mouth, I regretted them a little bit. I don't know why. Lewis was such a pain. But he seemed—I don't know, kind of pathetic. It must be tough leaving your friends, moving to a new town and starting a new school at the end of the year.

"Umm, how come you moved so late?" I asked Lewis, who looked as if he was going to cry.

"My mom got a job in Virginia. At first I was going to stay with my dad and finish school, but then—" He stopped and crumbled the rest of his cookie on the ground. "My dad didn't want me.

When my mom and dad got divorced, they split everything, even us kids. My brother went with Dad. Mom got me."

I couldn't blame Mr. Butler for picking Lewis's brother instead of Lewis. But still, it must have hurt. Maybe that was why Lewis acted the way he did. But just as I was about to say something nice, he started tearing up the little plants Mrs. Monicure had just planted.

"Stupid plants," he said. "Stupid garden. Stupid world."

"Stop it!" I yelled, slapping his hand. "Are you crazy?"

I thought he was going to slap me back, but he just gaped at me.

"Why do you have to be so mean, Lewis?" I said. "Nobody's done anything to you. Mrs. M. hasn't done anything to you, except be nice. And what do you do? You call her a witch and tear up her plants. You know how much she loves her plants."

A small voice interrupted our fight. "All witches love their plants," Oliver remarked. "They use them in their spells. I read it in a book, in the grown-up section of the library. The book told about the herbs and plants witches use."

"Oliver," I said, "forget about witches. Mrs. Monicure is not—"

Lewis suddenly jumped up. "Plants!" he cried, as if he'd just discovered gold. "I bet I know where the spells are! The only place we haven't looked!" He raced into the house with Oliver hard on his heels. I had to go after them, if only to keep Lewis out of trouble.

They were in the dining room. Lewis was taking plants off the white metal cart Mrs. Monicure rolled from window to window, to make sure her flowers got enough sun. The flowers were planted in thick clay pots with attached saucers.

Lewis stared at the plants he had lined up on the dining room table. One of the African violets was planted in a small pot that was tucked inside a larger pot. Carefully he lifted the violet out of the larger pot. He reached inside and pulled out a plastic envelope. I could see the faint spidery writing on the yellowed sheet of notebook paper folded inside the plastic.

We all held our breath as Lewis took the paper out and unfolded it. Leaning over Lewis's arm, Oliver read in a hushed voice the single word written at the top of the page, "Weathermaking."

Nobody spoke for a few seconds.

"It-it's just another of those household hint things," I said, breaking the silence.

"No, it isn't," Lewis said. "This is the whole enchilada, and you know it."

I snatched the paper away. The directions listed a lot of funny-sounding plants. "It's probably a...a...a...laundry recipe or something."

"You're wrong, Sandra!" Lewis crowed. "Wrong wrong wrong! I'll show you!" Lewis snatched the paper back. "Come on, Oliver. We're going to make a hurricane!"

I dashed after them. I had read what was written underneath the title, "Weathermaking." In tiny, tiny letters was the warning, "Management of wind and rain. *Use with caution.*" Lewis didn't know beans about managing wind and rain. And I knew he surely wouldn't use caution.

I found them in the garden. Lewis was reading the names of plants off the sheet while Oliver located them in the herb border. Oliver spent more time in the garden with Mrs. M. He knew a lot about plants and flowers.

"Henbane, pennyroyal, soapwart, Good King Henry," Lewis recited. "Got those?"

"I think so." Oliver pulled the last plant up gently by its roots and laid it neatly on the pile of other plants.

"You can't do this," I said.

Ignoring me, Lewis asked Oliver, "Is that it? Do we have them all?" Oliver nodded. They gathered the plants and went into the house.

I wondered if I should tell Mrs. Monicure that two of her after-school kids were about to brew up a hurricane. She would think I was nuts.

Mrs. Monicure was hanging up sheets on her long clothesline. "Nothing like April breezes to make bedclothes smell good," she said to me. "You can't get that smell in the dryer."

"Mrs. M.," I said, handing her a bunch of

wooden clothespins from the bag that bobbed from a hook on the line.

"Yes, Sandra?" She spoke through a clothespin clenched between her teeth as she tugged at a heavy quilt.

I glanced up at the blue sky. Not a cloud in sight. "Uh—think it'll rain?" I said limply.

Mrs. Monicure tipped her head back. "Doesn't look like it. The weatherman isn't calling for rain the rest of the week. I wish it would. My garden needs it, but it'll take something drastic for it to rain now, the way that sun is shining. Magic, maybe. Sandra? Are you all right? You look kind of funny."

"Probably. I mean, I'm fine." I backed toward the house. "I just have to go check on something." I broke into a run. In the kitchen, Lewis and Oliver were huddled around the stove. Lewis stirred green leaves and bits of flowers into a saucepan of greenish gunk.

"Throw that stuff out right now," I ordered. "Before—"

"Before what?" Lewis stopped stirring long

enough to glare at me. "You're the one who doesn't believe in spells and witches, remember? Scared, Sandra?"

"No, I'm not scared. You don't know what you're doing, Lewis. Anyway, Mrs. M. didn't give you permission to use her stove."

"Be quiet," he commanded. "I have to say this right." He looked at the paper propped up against a teapot. In a low voice he chanted, "Awake, oh North Wind, and come thou south, blow upon my garden, that the spices thereof may flow out."

We waited.

Nothing happened.

Then a bubble appeared on the surface of the greenish goo in the saucepan. The bubble popped, filling the kitchen with the most horrible stink in the world.

"Arrgghhh!" I gagged. "What's that smell?"

"Is it supposed to do that?" Oliver gasped.

Lewis bent over the pan and frowned. He tried to consult the spell paper, but the smell was too much for him. He staggered back, and the paper crumpled in his hand.

The stink wrapped around us like a blanket. We couldn't get away from it. I pinched my nose shut, but I could still smell it.

"Lewis, throw it out!" I cried. "You're going to kill us!"

A greenish cloud mushroomed over the pan and curled into the air like a fog made of pea soup. The smell became like a living thing, like a monster out of control. We couldn't stand it another second. We stumbled out and collapsed in a heap, gulping huge swallows of fresh air.

I wiped my eyes and wheezed. "Your spell was a big fat flop," I cried. All you made was the grossest smell in the world. Now who's wrong?"

Lewis opened his mouth to protest, when a drop of rain hit him—splat!—on the nose. Another drop of rain streaked Oliver's glasses.

"It's raining!" Lewis shrieked.

I looked up. A small dark cloud hung over Mrs. M.'s garden. The rest of the sky was as blue as ever. Rain slanted from the cloud, sprinkling Mrs. M.'s garden and yard and us. But the street in front of her house was as dry as a bone.

"It's only raining here," Oliver said.

Lewis leaped up and danced around. "I did it! I did it! I made it rain!"

By now the stink-cloud had oozed out the window, reaching green fingers through the screen. Mrs. Monicure came running from the rain, carrying wet sheets and blankets.

"Sandra! Lewis! What's that terrible smell?" she cried. She hurried into the house and came out an instant later with the pan bundled in a tea towel. She threw the gunk into the garbage can.

"Scorched," she said, staring at the blackened bottom of her pan. "My best pan, ruined." She looked at us. "You know I don't mind you using the stove, but only when I'm around. What in the world were you cooking, anyway?"

"Uhh, hot chocolate," I said quickly.

"I never knew chocolate could make a stink like *that*," Mrs. M. said, shaking her head. She wiped raindrops off her sleeve. "I could have sworn it wasn't going to rain today, or I wouldn't have washed bedclothes. But I'm not complaining. My garden surely could use it." She went inside to the kitchen.

Lewis and Oliver were rolling around on the rain-soaked grass, wrestling and fooling around.

"San-dra," Lewis taunted. "*Now* who's wrong?"

"It's not exactly a hurricane," I snapped. "And it was probably going to rain anyway."

The spell paper was lying on the wet grass. Somebody had to put it back before Mrs. Monicure missed it. Picking up the paper, I stalked into the house.

Mrs. Monicure was running hot water in her scorched saucepan. I tiptoed past the door. I could put the spell paper back in the flowerpot without her seeing me.

As I lifted the pot and replaced the paper in the plastic envelope, I wondered what was really going on. This spell couldn't have worked. It couldn't really be magic. And Mrs. M. couldn't really be a witch, could she?

When I turned around to go back outside, I jumped. I saw Shadow staring right at me. Maybe it was my imagination, but it seemed as if the cat had the strangest look in his eyes.

Five

"THERE'S going to be a full moon in two nights," Oliver said, closing the almanac. "Friday."

We were sitting around the dining room table a week later. Mrs. Monicure was in the kitchen, as usual, but she couldn't hear us. At least I didn't *think* she could hear us.

Lewis had checked a farmer's almanac out of the school library. He told Oliver, his willing slave, to look up when the next full moon was, while he helped himself to the plate of mini-pizzas Mrs. Monicure had fixed for us—*all* of us, though Lewis was definitely taking the pig's share.

"Friday? Good," Lewis said with his mouth

62

full reaching for his fourth mini-pizza. "You know what *that* means."

"No," I said, "what does it mean?"

"A witch's powers are strongest on a full moon," Lewis explained. "Remember, we read about it. Their powers are really strong at midnight. I bet Mrs. M. has a witch meeting that night. That's when they meet, once a month, at the full moon. See Sandra, *I* do my homework."

He meant homework on witches. But that was a dig at me. Actually, right then I *was* doing homework, real homework, not witch business. Mr. Crowley told me that I couldn't go to the Redskins assembly on Friday unless I turned in a list of ideas for my write-a-book project. I wasn't crazy about football, but a real player from the Washington Redskins team was coming to talk to our school, and I didn't want to miss it. Anyway, I'd get out of math.

"Does Mrs. Monicure have a calendar?" Lewis asked Oliver. "The kind she writes doctors appointments and stuff like that on?"

"Yeah. It's on the back of the door to the

basement," Oliver replied. "Want me to get it?"

I watched Oliver practically break his neck to get the calendar. He would do anything for Lewis. Ever since Lewis brewed up the rain shower that day, Oliver thought Lewis Butler was the greatest thing since sliced bread.

My opinion of Lewis hadn't changed, though I had started to wonder a little about our baby-sitter now. The rainstorm couldn't have happened just because Lewis threw some weeds in a pot and mumbled a poem over it...could it? I mean, isn't there a law in physics that says it's impossible to cook up a storm in a saucepan?

Oliver came running back with the calendar. The calendar had a picture of fuzzy kittens in a basket on the top half. The days in the bottom half were marked in big squares. Mrs. Monicure had jotted her appointments: "Dentist," "Tax Man," "Hospital Bazaar." The last one was for tomorrow. She was in the kitchen now, making brownies for the bake sale.

Lewis stuck his finger on the square for the coming Friday. It was blank. "She didn't write it down," he said.

I put my pencil down. "Do you really think she'd put 'Night out with Witches' on her calendar? Lewis, you are bonkers. It's not like going bowling!"

"Well, that's when they meet," he said. "On the full moon, witches get together. Their powers are at a peak then. They probably do all kinds of magic stuff."

"They meet in a coven," Oliver said. "That's what a group of witches is called. There are 13 witches in a coven."

"Mrs. M. will meet her witch friends Friday at midnight," Lewis said.

"So? How will we know what she does?" I asked.

"I, uh, have to think about that some more," he said, chomping on another mini-pizza. I guess food helped him think better. He looked over at my smeary piece of paper. "Haven't you finished that list yet?"

"I can't dream up ideas on the spot. Look at these and tell me if any of them will make a good story." I pushed the paper to his side of the table.

He read my list out loud, with a mouth full of pizza. "'Space invader comes to Centreville,''Bank robbers under the bed,' 'Indiana Jones finds lost treasure.'"

I stared nervously at the pitcher of Kool-Aid in the center of the table. Lewis was a pest, but he did get good grades in school, even when he didn't cheat. He had something I would never have—imagination.

"Are they any good?" I asked in a little voice.

His answer was a groan. "Sandra, you can't write about Indiana Jones. That's a movie."

"They make movies from books all the time. Why can't I make a book from a movie?"

"You just can't. Bank robbers under the bed? How could that be a book? The space invader is good, but what do you know about aliens?"

"I know one when I see one," I said.

He crossed his eyes. "Very funny. Forget this made-up stuff. You don't know anything about bank robbers or lost treasures or space invaders. Write about what you know. I've been doing these write-a-book projects since third grade, and that's what one teacher told me, 'Write what you know.' That way you won't get stuck."

I looked at him. "But I don't *know* anything!"

He shrugged. "Sorry, I can't help you there."

I wanted to hit him. But deep down inside, I figured he was right. I wadded up the list. Scratch the Redskins assembly, I thought. I was going to spend that period in Mr. Crowley's room.

Oliver wasn't interested in my problems with school. "Have you thought of anything yet?" he asked Lewis. "About Friday? My mom'll be here any minute. She's picking me up early today."

"Are you guys going out?" I said.

"I'm not. *She* is." He pushed his glasses up on his nose. I could tell he wasn't happy about it, but I didn't want to pry.

"Your mom's going out on a date? Who with?" nosy Lewis demanded.

Oliver slumped in his chair. "This guy from work. She says it's not a date. They're just going out to eat. But *I'm* not going with them. Not that I would, even if they begged me."

"Sounds like a date to me." Lewis hummed a few bars of "Here Comes the Bride."

I glared at him. "It's not funny."

"I can't believe she's going out with some-body—else," Oliver said in a small voice. "Doesn't she miss my daddy anymore? I still do."

No one spoke for a moment. Even obnoxious, big-mouth Lewis didn't have a smart remark.

I couldn't imagine what it must feel like to have my father die. I didn't think Lewis could, either. Even though he probably didn't see his father very much since the divorce, at least he knew his dad was still alive.

"Okay," he said dramatically. "Guess what we are going to do Friday night."

"What?" Oliver leaned forward, his sadness gone for the moment.

"We're going to follow Mrs. Monicure. To her witch meeting. At midnight." He grinned at both of us. We stared back at him.

In the kitchen, Mrs. M. sang a country-and-western song off-key. Was it possible that a lady who baked brownies for the hospital bazaar and sang corny songs would join a group of witches under a full moon?

I didn't know what to believe anymore. After the day Lewis found the weathermaking spell and cooked up an unscheduled April shower, I guess I was almost ready to believe anything.

* * * * *

Oliver didn't meet us at the door the next day. He just sat in front of Mrs. M.'s television, watching a cartoon. And he didn't even like cartoons.

Mrs. Monicure served us our snack in the kitchen. "Oliver's upset," she told us. "His mother went out to dinner last night with a fellow. And she's going out again tomorrow night. I know because his mother called me today and asked if I could come over and stay with Oliver. I said I would love to, but I had plans myself for tomorrow night."

Lewis kicked my shin. Behind Mrs. M.'s back, he made a witch face. I kicked him back.

"I gave her the number of another babysitter.

A nice girl." She sighed, running her fingers through her gray hair. "Poor kid. It's so hard losing a parent at his age. Of course his mother wants to date again. She's still a young woman. Oliver just can't understand that."

Lewis didn't seem to hear a word she said. He was ogling the necklace Mrs. M. wore around her neck. When she left the room to answer the phone, he muttered to me, "What is that thing she's wearing? It's weird."

It *was* a little weird. The necklace had feathers tied to a yellow silk cord. No beads or stones or anything, just feathers. She didn't wear it very often. Once I asked her about it, and she said a friend who lived in Peru made it for her.

"It was a present from a friend in Peru," I explained. "It's probably an Indian necklace or something."

Mrs. Monicure was talking pretty loud on the phone. Whoever had called must have been hard of hearing. Lewis and I could listen in.

"Yes," she said, "I'll be there. No, I won't be late this time. All right. See you tomorrow night."

Lewis jabbed my arm.

"Will you quit poking me?" I cried, exasperated. "I'm not your punching bag, Lewis."

"Sorry." For a change, he sounded as if he really meant it. "Did you hear that? She said she'd see somebody tomorrow night! I told you! Probably one of her witch friends."

"Lewis," I said, "she could be seeing *anybody* tomorrow night. It doesn't have to be a witch."

"I bet it is. Get Oliver. I'll meet you guys in the garden. We have to make plans."

Oliver didn't want to come with me. "I'm watching this," he said.

I switched off the television. "This is witch business." That got him moving.

Lewis had hogged the best chair in the garden. Shadow was curled at his feet, his eyes like yellow marbles in the dappled sunshine. Lewis opened his school notebook to a clean page. At the top of the paper, he wrote *Operation Witchbuster*. Then he divided the rest of the page into columns and wrote our names at the head of each column.

"Okay," he said. "The only way we'll ever prove 100 percent that Mrs. M. is a witch is to see her in action—doing witch stuff with a bunch of other witches. We have to follow her tomorrow night. She'll lead us to her witch meeting. And we'll see her become a real witch." He pointed to me. "Sandra, what are you going to bring?"

"Bring? What are you talking about?"

"This is a dangerous expedition. We'll need supplies." When I looked blank, he yelled, "Food, dummy!"

"Don't call me dummy!" I yelled back. "What do you want me to bring? Cookies? Sandwiches? Beef Wellington?"

"Sandwiches will be fine. No peanut butter." Lewis wrote down *sandwiches* by my name. "Cookies would be great, too."

"Any particular kind, Your Majesty?"

"I like any kind of cookie," Lewis said. "What about you, squirt? What can you bring?"

"How about something to drink?" Oliver said.

"Good." Lewis entered *soda* by Oliver's name on the chart.

"What about *you*, mastermind?" I asked.

"I'll bring equipment," he replied. "Flash-lights, a compass, rope, stuff like that."

"What are we going to do—tie her up and make Mrs. Monicure confess that she rides a broom?" I said, smirking.

"You don't care, do you?" Lewis said, firing back. "You don't care about school. You don't care that your babysitter is a witch. You don't care about anything."

"I do too!" What did he know about me?

"Are we really going to follow Mrs. M. to her witch meeting?" Oliver asked. The sad look had left his face. He looked interested again.

"You bet." Lewis stuck the pencil behind his ear. "Here's the plan. Tomorrow night, we'll meet on the corner. We'll hide in those bushes—" he pointed to the lilac shrubs by the front door, "—and wait for her to come out. Then follow her."

"Suppose she jumps in her car," I said. "How can we follow her in a car if we're on foot?"

"She won't use her car," Lewis said. "I never heard of a witch driving to a witch meeting."

"But you don't know."

"Sandra, where do *you* think the meeting will be? In a restaurant? It'll have to be in the woods or in a field someplace, where the witches can do their magic. She won't drive."

"Okay. So what are we going to do again?" I asked. "And why do we need all that stuff?"

"We'll meet on the corner at, umm, 11:15. Then we'll follow Mrs. M. wherever she goes. We'll need the compass so that we can find our way back. And the flashlights because it will be dark. Probably the meeting place won't be too close. We might be walking a long time and we'll get hungry and thirsty. Or we might even wait until we're at the meeting place and then hide behind a rock or something and eat while we watch the witches."

Lewis dropped his voice to a whisper.

"Can you imagine what we'll see? A whole bunch of witches—"

"A coven," Oliver said.

"—yeah, a coven, dancing in the moonlight, all wearing black dresses. They might even fly their brooms. It'll be so spooky."

75

Shivering, I closed my eyes. Lewis could make me see those witches leaping and jumping in the moonlight. I pictured their black capes flapping as they flew their brooms above the trees. And Mrs. Monicure, our sitter, was one of them.

"It sounds scary," Oliver said.

I opened my eyes and looked at him. Oliver was a little kid, almost two years younger than Lewis and I. He couldn't sneak out in the middle of the night and follow Mrs. M. to her witch meeting. It would be scary enough for *me* to do.

"You can't go," I told him. "You're too young."

"I am not!" he said in protest. "I want to see Mrs. Monicure be a witch. You can't stop me!"

I said to Lewis. "Tell him he's too young. His mother will kill him if she catches him sneaking out of the house." I hated to think what my parents would do if they caught me.

Oliver clenched his fists. "You can't make me stay home. I'm going. Nobody will know I'm gone. My mother has a date. That dumb old babysitter will never know."

I was worrying about how I'd sneak out of my

own house with a sack of food at 11:00. Lewis and his crazy plans.

"Scared?" Lewis asked me, half-teasing.

He knew how to get my goat every time. Standing, I brushed dirt off my jeans. "I'll be on the corner at 11:15," I said. "With sandwiches. No peanut butter."

Just then, Shadow got up, too. He arched his back in a stretch that made him look like a cat on a Halloween card. He blinked at me with his yellow eyes as if he knew exactly what we were up to.

Six

"**D**O we have any brownies or cupcakes?" I asked my mother the next morning.

Mom checked the goodie cupboard. "All we have are a few stale vanilla wafers," she said. "I need to go to the store this afternoon. Do you need cupcakes for school?"

"Not exactly," I answered. "More like for after school." That wasn't true either, but I don't think my mother would have been thrilled to hear that I needed cupcakes for a midnight picnic. "Will you buy a brownie mix today?" I asked. Microwave mixes were a cinch to make. Mom said she would.

As I got ready to catch the bus, Mom asked, "Do you have your homework, Sandra?"

"We didn't have any. *Honest.* Mr. Crowley doesn't give us homework every single night."

"Even so, you should be working on your projects. If you fall behind, you'll never catch up. Your father and I and Mr. Crowley all agree you can do the work. You just won't for some reason." She kissed my cheek. "Bye. Have a good day."

As if I could have a good day with that cheery message ringing in my ears and the prospect of what was ahead of me that evening.

I didn't see Lewis until lunch time. He never rode the bus in the morning. His mother drove him to school on her way to her job.

Lewis was waiting for me when I left the food line with my tray. "I got three flashlights," he said, "and a compass and a mess kit."

I put my tray at the end of an empty table. He sat down across from me. "Lewis, we aren't really going through with this, are we?" I asked.

"I knew you'd wimp out," he said with a sneer.

"I'm not wimping out!" I answered. "It's crazy! Sneak out of our houses in the middle of the night and walk over to Mrs. Monicure's house and follow her to who-knows-where." Kids were staring at me. I lowered my voice. "It's worse than crazy. It's *suicide!*"

He stuck his finger in my pudding cup and licked it. "It's the only way to catch Mrs. M. in the act. She'll have to do something witchy at a witch meeting."

I grabbed my pudding away before he could swipe another fingerful. "What if we get caught? What if Mrs. Monicure doesn't leave her house tonight?"

"She will."

"What if she leaves before we get there? Suppose she walks miles and miles and miles? How will we get back?"

Lewis just smiled. "You don't have to go," he said. "Oliver and I will go by ourselves. We don't want any scaredy-cats along."

Ugghh. He had me over a barrel, and he knew it. If I didn't go, Oliver would think I wasn't as brave as Lewis. It would be Lewis and Oliver against chicken Cassandra from now on.

I had to go.

* * * * *

For someone who had to attend a witch meeting that night, Mrs. Monicure seemed awfully calm. She gave us big dishes of vanilla, strawberry, and chocolate ice cream with chocolate candy sprinkled on top, and then settled down with a new romance novel.

"I've worked in my garden all day," she said, easing herself into the stuffed chair with a sigh. "Oh, my aching back."

"You'll be able to. . .uh, do whatever you were going to do, won't you?" Lewis jiggled his spoon, looking worried.

Mrs. Monicure peered at him over the half-glasses she wore to read. "It's nice of you kids to be so concerned. I'm fine—I just overdid it today, that's all. Why don't you go out and enjoy the sunshine when you're finished?"

"Good idea," I said, scraping my bowl. Lewis was acting weird, even for him. Better to get him outside before he let something slip about tonight, I thought.

"Is there going to be a full moon tonight?" he asked innocently enough.

Mrs. M. thought a moment. "I think there is."

"You know what *that* means," Lewis said, arching his eyebrows.

"No, what?" Mrs. M. looked puzzled.

I grabbed Lewis by the collar. "Uh, nothing. He's delirious because we had to run the 600 in gym today. The sun fried his brain."

In the garden, Lewis imitated a witch cackle. "I almost had her, didn't I?"

"No, you didn't. Mrs. M. thinks you're nuts, and so do I."

"I don't," Oliver said. He sat at Lewis's feet, his slave for life.

"Oliver," I said, "you really should stay home tonight." It was bad enough that Lewis and I were making this suicide mission.

"I'm going with you," Oliver insisted.

"Let's synchronize our watches," Lewis said. "In about. . .eight hours, we'll meet on the corner. Operation Witchbuster will begin!"

* * * * *

No one was waiting under the streetlamp on the corner. My watch said exactly 11:15. Setting the duffel bag on the sidewalk, I leaned against the post and jammed my hands in my jeans pockets. Even though it was April, it was chilly at night. If Lewis didn't show up—I couldn't think of enough awful things to do to him.

Then he was there. "Did you have any trouble getting out?" he asked.

"No." My parents were in the den, watching a movie on cable. I just slipped out the front door. They never heard me leave. And since I keep my bedroom door closed at night, I knew they wouldn't check on me until morning.

"My mom almost caught me." Lewis pretended to wipe sweat off his forehead. "She came out of her room just as I was opening the front door. I ducked behind the sofa real quick. Then I had to wait until she went back in her room." He glanced around. "Where's Oliver?" he asked.

"Home asleep, I hope." I still thought Oliver was too young to be out late at night. So were we, for that matter.

"She hasn't come out yet, has she?" Lewis said. We could see Mrs. Monicure's house. Lights glowed in the living room and the kitchen. Lewis checked his watch. "She has to be at the witch meeting by midnight. It can't be too far."

Suddenly a small figure darted out of the bushes. I screamed.

"Cool it," Lewis said. "It's only the kid."

Oliver clutched a thermos bottle to his chest. "I made it!" In the streetlight's glow, his face was pale and ghostly. But his eyes were shining with excitement.

"Did anybody see you?" I asked anxiously.

"Are you kidding? That babysitter wouldn't notice if a bomb went off. All she does is yak on the phone to her boyfriend." Oliver held up the thermos and said, "I brought juice. Is that okay? We didn't have any soda."

I nudged the canvas duffel with my toe. "I brought bologna sandwiches. *And* I made brownies. You guys better eat every crumb, because I'm not going to lug—"

"Move it! Here she comes!" Lewis dragged me into the bushes. Oliver scurried behind us, carrying the thermos and duffel bag.

Thorny twigs snagged my hair, and my arm hurt where Lewis grabbed me. But I forgot about all that as I watched Mrs. Monicure come out her front door. Even though it was dark, I could tell she had on her beige coat. No black cape. No pointy hat. She switched on the porch light and locked her door behind her. Then she walked quickly down the sidewalk. It was clear she was going someplace important.

"Stay back," Lewis ordered as Oliver and I lurched after her. "Don't get too close. If she turns around, she'll see us. Just keep her in sight."

We crept behind the hedges and bushes along the sidewalk, hunched over like people in a spy movie. We followed Mrs. Monicure for three blocks. My back began to hurt from running in a crouch. If we had to travel much farther like that, I would have to go home in a wheelchair.

85

"Where do you think she's going?" I said to Lewis, panting.

"The woods," he answered. "Remember that book? Witches hold their meetings in the woods."

I remembered a drawing of black-caped witches dancing in the moonlight in a clearing of trees.

Oliver said, "If she's going to the woods, she's walking the wrong way."

That was true. The houses were getting closer together, and we passed small shopping centers. Mrs. Monicure was definitely heading into town.

"I sure didn't need this stuff," Lewis said, hooking his flashlight to his belt. Two more flashlights and a rattling canteen dangled from loops. Streetlamps cast bright pools of light on the sidewalk. We sure weren't going to get lost.

Suddenly, Lewis threw out his arms. Oliver and I ran into him. "She's going in that building," Lewis said in a hiss.

The low brick building was lit with strong spotlights. More lights glared at the big windows. Cars packed the graveled parking lot. When Mrs.

Monicure opened the double door at the entrance, we could hear rock music and laughter.

"Sounds like a party," Oliver said.

"I don't get it." Lewis squinted at the sign over the door. "What is this place, anyway?"

"The community center," I told him. "Mom comes here for lectures sometimes. And Dad brought me here last Fourth of July to see the fireworks. There's always something going on."

The three of us looked at each other. A witch meeting in the town community center? The whole idea was too far-fetched for me. "She's probably going to that party," I said. "A perfectly normal party with perfectly normal people having perfectly normal fun."

"We'll see," Lewis said. He signaled for us to creep along the driveway behind him. We sneaked up to the door and peered inside. A long hallway stretched the length of the building. Teenagers spilled from a big room to the right, laughing and dancing to the music. Mrs. M. couldn't be in that crowd, I thought. But there were other rooms down the hall, behind closed doors.

No one noticed as we snaked around the partly open door and slipped past the party room.

"We can't just barge into these rooms," I whispered hoarsely to Lewis.

"No, but we can listen." He flattened his ear to the first door on the left. He shook his head. "Nobody in that one," he whispered.

We tried each of the doors. The last one on the left was partially opened. *This one*, Lewis mouthed. Lining up like animals on a totem pole—Lewis on top, me in the middle, Oliver on the bottom—we put one eye to the opening and looked inside.

I don't know what we expected. Maybe to see a bunch of old crones with warts on their noses dancing around a big, bubbling kettle and black cats flying on broomsticks. What we saw looked like an ordinary ladies' club meeting.

There were no windows in the room, but bright travel posters decorated the walls. Five or six tables with fold-up chairs were grouped in the middle. On a smaller table, refreshments were laid out—green punch and plates of cookies.

The ladies were dressed like Mrs. Monicure—neat slacks and flowered tops and sweaters. They were mostly gray-haired, but some were younger.

Two women showed each other pictures of their grandchildren. They oohed and aahed over the snapshots. Mrs. Monicure, who sat with her back to us, was giving another lady instructions on how to crochet a crib blanket. Other women exchanged recipes.

A lady with silver-framed glasses told them to find their places. The women chose seats at the tables. Some set up Scrabble boards. Others shuffled cards.

I drew back from the door. "Some spooky witch meeting," I whispered.

Lewis whispered back, "Did you count them? There are 13. That's the number in a witch meeting."

"Look," Oliver said. We pressed our faces to the opened door.

The woman with the silver-framed glasses was dealing cards at her table. *But not with her hands!* The cards just flew off the shuffled deck and landed in front of the other women. They calmly picked up the cards and arranged them into fans as if cards sailed at them every day of the week.

I couldn't believe my eyes. Was this real magic? It had to be a trick. But I wondered if my father, the physics teacher, had a law that explained sailing cards.

We sat cross-legged on the floor next to the door, our mouths gaping. Maybe Mrs. M. was in a magic club, the kind that does tricks for kids at hospitals and stuff like that. These normal-looking grandmothers couldn't be witches!

Lewis made motions that he was hungry. Careful not to make any noise, I took sandwiches and brownies from the duffel. Oliver passed around the thermos. As we ate, we listened.

"Does the Midsummer Committee have anything to report?" asked the lady with the silver glasses. I figured she was the club leader.

A woman next to Mrs. M. studied her cards before replying, "The quarry site is fine. It has been abandoned for years. So we won't be bothered. I propose we meet there next month, too."

"Does anyone second the motion?" asked Silver Glasses.

Several ladies seconded the motion.

"Passed," Silver Glasses announced after the vote. "We will meet at the quarry for our May meeting." Then she asked, "When does the next full moon fall?"

A woman in a pink sweater consulted a calendar. "May 23. At that meeting, I'll have a sign-up sheet for new spells to be performed on Midsummer's Eve," she said.

Lewis punched my shoulder. Spells! There was no denying what the lady said. Was Lewis right after all? Were these ladies really witches?

Silver Glasses spoke to Mrs. Monicure. "Would you like to to renew your membership this year, Amelia?"

We couldn't see Mrs. M.'s face, but her back suddenly stiffened, as if she was embarrassed. "I don't know," she mumbled. "I really want to be back in the group again—as a full member. I miss Midsummer and All Hallows—we have such fun.

But my spells...I just can't seem..." Her voice trailed off.

Silver Glasses clucked her tongue and said in a kindly voice, "Won't you try again, Amelia. We'd love to have you back full-time. Well, does anyone have a new spell this month?"

"I do," a plump, yellow-haired woman said. "Watch this." She stood and stared hard at the punch bowl. For a while nothing happened. But then, slowly, the punch changed color, going from green to purple!

Nobody had touched the punch bowl. It couldn't have been a trick. I saw it with my own eyes. It was magic! That was the only explanation. The tingly feeling in my spine grew stronger. We really were watching witches at a witch meeting—witches who could make cards fly and change the color of punch!

"I wonder if it tastes like grape now," Lewis said.

The other ladies clapped. Yellow Hair smiled.

"Very pretty," commented Silver Glasses. "Anyone else?" When no one volunteered, Silver

Glasses shook her head. "It's not like the old days. Remember when we met every week? And we all had new spells at every meeting?"

"Nobody has that much energy anymore!" said the older lady next to Mrs. Monicure. They laughed.

Silver Glasses got up. "I think I smell bologna. Time for refreshments, ladies."

We scrambled away from the door, snatching the remains of our picnic. She had smelled our bologna sandwiches!

Down the hall, Lewis said, "It's way after midnight. We better get back home." The teenage party in the big room was still in full swing. We ran out the door and into the parking lot.

"We have to take Oliver home first," I said to Lewis. "It's too late for him to be out by himself."

We set off toward Oliver's house. "Did you see that lady with the cards? And the purple punch? I *knew* there'd be magic!" Lewis said.

For once, I couldn't argue. I had seen it all with my own eyes. It looked as if Lewis was right after all. "What was that business about the quarry and Midsummer?" I asked.

Oliver replied, "Midsummer's Eve is a big night for witches. It's the longest day of the year. Another special night is Halloween."

"They must be planning to have their meeting at a quarry," Lewis put in. "But Mrs. M. can't go. They said she's not a full member."

"I wonder why? The others liked her," I said.

"Probably her spells don't work," Lewis suggested. "Remember that time with the salt? She could barely make it appear."

"I hope she gets back in the group," Oliver said. "I could tell she was sad about it."

A breeze rattled the bare branches above our heads. The limbs seemed like claws reaching out for us.

Lewis stopped and looked at us in a funny way. He whispered, "Those ladies were *real* witches. I-I don't know if I ever really believed it, but ..."

Then we all started to run. And it wasn't just because we were cold. We were a little scared, and we all wanted to be home.

"Do you think your mother's still out?" I asked, out of breath, as we raced down Oliver's street. "Let's hope the babysitter hasn't figured out you're gone."

"She's probably still on the phone," Oliver said. "Mom said she wouldn't be home until late."

We got our answer when we got close to the house. Every single light was on. And Mrs. Cantrell's car was in the driveway.

Seven

"UH-OH," Oliver said. "Mom's home. I guess the babysitter missed me?"

"We have to walk him to the door," I told Lewis. "His mom won't be so worried if she knows he was with us."

Lewis shook his head. "Are you crazy? Oliver's mother will call our folks, and then we'll *all* be in trouble."

I should have known Lewis would wimp out. He was brave around witches, but he wouldn't stand up for his friends in a million years.

"I'll go with you," I said to Oliver. "At least *one* of us is your real friend."

"No, I'll go by myself," Oliver said. "No point in you guys getting in trouble." His voice trembled, but he squared his shoulders as he marched up the driveway. He turned back once. "See you guys on Monday."

"Let's beat it," Lewis said, taking off. We ran without stopping until we reached my corner.

"See you in school," Lewis called to me.

I didn't answer. If I never saw that rat again it would be too soon. The den light was still on in my house. My mother had gone to bed, but Dad was still up marking papers. No one had bothered to check the front door—it was still unlocked. I eased inside, holding my breath. Then I sneaked down the hall to my bedroom. Safe!

I crawled between the covers without changing into my pajamas. I was so tired! I lay there thinking about witches and magic spells and flying cards and purple punch. Then I fell asleep, as if someone had cast a spell over me.

* * * * *

Lewis was wrong about one thing. We all got in trouble anyway.

Dad was at the hardware store, but Mom had my breakfast and a sharp look for me when I went into the kitchen. "What's wrong with you this morning?" she asked, setting toast and cereal in front of me.

"Uhh, nothing." That was a lie. I could barely move, I was so exhausted. But I had to cover it up. I couldn't tell Mom I was too pooped to lift my spoon because I'd been out half the night at a witch meeting.

"You have dark circles under your eyes," Mom said. "Didn't you sleep well?"

"No." Then I added, to throw her off the track, "I guess it's all these end-of-the-year projects we have in school."

My mother sat down with a sigh. "Sandra, tell me what's going on at Mrs. Monicure's."

I dropped my spoon. How did she know?

"Oliver's mother called me this morning. She said Oliver sneaked out of the house last night and didn't come home until after midnight. He told her that he was out trying to prove Mrs. Monicure was a witch! Mrs. Cantrell is very upset, naturally. Oliver has never done anything like this. She's ready to look for another after-school sitter. What do you know about this?"

I *knew* Oliver was too young to go with us. His mother obviously must have gotten him to confess. I wasn't going to admit the truth about Mrs. Monicure being a witch. But I had no problem with squealing on that rat Lewis.

"It's Lewis Butler," I said. "He's the cause of this. He makes up stories and Oliver believes him. It's all Lewis's fault."

"But to sneak out of the house in the middle of the night!" Mom said. "Oliver's just a little boy. Surely, you older children are more responsible than to lead that child on."

"It wasn't me!" I cried. "It was *Lewis.* He's been causing trouble ever since he came. I wish he'd go away! Can't Mrs. Monicure get rid of him? Then it'll be like it was before, just me and Oliver and Mrs. Monicure."

My mother didn't answer. She just cleared the table. The weekend dragged by. I was anxious for Monday to come so that I could talk to Oliver and find out what happened.

But I saw Lewis first. He cornered me as our classes filed down the hall to recess on Monday morning. "How'd it go Friday night?" he asked.

"What do you care?" I said with a growl.

"Boy, are you grumpy if you miss a little sleep." He lowered his voice. "I found out where the quarry is. It's not too far from Mrs. M.'s. I'll show you how I found it after school, okay?"

I glared at him. "You just don't get it, do you? You're not even worried about what happened to Oliver. All you care about is this dumb witch business!"

"He got home okay," Lewis said. "And what did you want me to do, go in with him and hold his hand? And have his mother yell at me? And *my* mother too? Everybody babies that kid too much. Let him grow up a little."

Mrs. Griffin, Lewis's teacher, blew her whistle for her class to line up. Lewis hustled over.

But his last remark made me think. Oliver really didn't want us to go in with him Friday night. He wanted to face his mother alone. Maybe

Lewis was right. Maybe it was time to let Oliver grow up.

But what about Lewis? When was *he* going to grow up?

* * * * *

When we arrived at Mrs. Monicure's house that afternoon, she was sitting on the sofa absently petting Shadow. "Oliver's mother wants to send him to another sitter," Mrs. M. announced. "She says he's not happy here. And she has called your mother, Sandra, and yours, Lewis. She thinks you two should leave as well. I don't understand...I thought you children were happy here with me."

"We *are* happy!" I said. "I don't want to leave! I want to stay with you forever!"

"Me too," said Oliver. He was slouched in the chair, his glasses halfway down his nose. He looked too unhappy to push them up.

"Well, your parents have different ideas," Mrs. Monicure said. "They feel that you'd be better off with another sitter. I've really enjoyed having you kids here. Yes, I need the money your parents pay me to watch you. But it's more than that—we're sort of like a little family." Gently pushing the cat off her lap, she heaved herself to her feet. "You're probably hungry. I'll fix you something to eat."

When she went out to the kitchen, I turned on Lewis. "This is all your fault!" I said. "See what you've done! Now we'll all have to leave!"

He tried to dump the blame on Oliver. "What did you tell your mom the truth for? Couldn't you make anything up, for Pete's sake?"

Oliver stood up to him. "I read that if you tell people the truth, they usually don't believe it. Especially if it's something crazy, like what we did. I figured Mom wouldn't believe it and would yell at me, and that would be it. I didn't mention you guys at all."

"Mrs. M. didn't say *why* your mother wants to take you to another sitter," Lewis reasoned. "So she doesn't know *we* know she's a witch."

"Shhhh," I warned.

Mrs. M. came back in, bringing us each a big piece of chocolate cake. I felt so guilty that I could hardly eat mine. We just had to think of a way to help Mrs. Monicure.

"Let's go outside," Lewis said when we were finished. "I want to show you guys what I found."

In the garden, Lewis pulled a folded paper from his pocket and spread it on the ground. It was a map with squiggly lines and circles.

"This is a topographical map," he explained. "It shows hills and creeks and stuff. The real estate lady gave it to us when we moved here." He pointed to a square. "This is Mrs. Monicure's block. And this—" his finger moved a few inches over "—is the quarry. This is where the witches are going to meet next month. And on Midsummer's Eve."

"So?" I said.

"Want to go see it?" he asked. "It's not very far. Just a few streets over and through the woods."

"Lewis, what have you got in your head? Sawdust?" I tapped his head as if thumping a watermelon. "We just missed getting in the trouble of our lives last time. And now you want to get us in trouble *again.*"

"What's the big deal?" he asked.

"We're not allowed to leave Mrs. Monicure's property," Oliver said. "Not while she's supposed to be watching us."

Lewis snorted. "She's either in the kitchen or in the garden. She doesn't even know where we are half the time."

"We're not supposed to go past that fence—" Oliver began, but I cut him off.

"No, wait." Here was the way to solve our problem, to get Lewis thrown out, once and for all. We were sure to get caught leaving Mrs. Monicure's property. I would say Lewis made us, and that it was all his idea. Mrs. M. would tell our parents, and our folks would see that Lewis was the troublemaker. He would have to leave. And *we* could stay with Mrs. Monicure.

"I changed my mind," I said. "I'll go with you to the quarry." I knew Oliver would go along with whatever I did.

"All right!" Lewis cheered. "Coming, kid?"

Oliver gave me a nervous look, but he followed us out of the garden. We squirmed under the fence, and then cut through back yards until we reached the woods. We were puffing and sweaty by the time we came to a clearing.

"Just over this hill," Lewis cried. He ran ahead of us up the hill, whooping like an Indian in the movies. "Hey, you guys! Come see!"

Oliver and I scrambled to the top of the hill. We looked out over high cliffs of gray stone that dropped straight down to a murky green pool. Trees all around hid the quarry, like a secret the woods were keeping.

"I bet that pool is a thousand feet deep," Lewis said.

"Yeah," I said. "Why is this here?"

Oliver, who seemed to know a little bit about everything, replied, "It's an old gravel quarry. A long time ago, people dug big rocks out of that pit and crushed them to make little rocks. Gravel. Like you put on your driveway."

"Come on," said Lewis. "Let's see if we can find the place where the witches will meet."

As we walked down the sloping hillside, Oliver told us what he found out from the book he had read. Witches like to dance in a ring, going in the opposite direction of the sun's movement around the earth. They dance around a landmark, a stone or something. Near the entrance to the quarry, we found a pyramid-shaped boulder.

"This is it, I bet," Oliver said, patting the rock. "This would be a great rock to dance around."

I shivered, imagining those ladies singing and dancing in this deserted spot. I liked them better when they were showing each other pictures of their grandchildren and swapping recipes.

Then it struck me. If Mrs. Monicure wasn't a witch, we wouldn't have found out that she could make magic. And we wouldn't be in trouble and we wouldn't have to leave.

"Why do they have to be witches, anyway?" I said. "Why can't they just be themselves?"

"They probably like it," Oliver answered. "Mrs. Monicure isn't mean, like the witches in cartoons and fairy tales. She's nice. She helps people. She's a good witch."

"She might be a good witch," Lewis said, "but I don't think she's very good at it. I mean, her spells probably flop. That's why she's not a full member of their group. I wish we could help her get back in the group."

I stared at him. "You really mean it?"

"Well, yeah," he said. "Mrs. M. is okay." He looked embarrassed to admit he actually liked our babysitter. "Hey, let's explore!" he said.

He took off around the edge of the quarry. Oliver was right behind him. They picked up rocks and yelled to each other. Lewis pitched stones into the greenish pool. Oliver copied him. I guess boys were more interested in things like a big hole in the ground. Me, I couldn't see the fascination.

I sat on a log and thought about my plan to get rid of Lewis. The only reason I came to the quarry was to prove to the grownups that Lewis was the cause of all the trouble. I wanted our parents to see that he was no good and make him find another after-school sitter.

But as I sat and watched Lewis and Oliver

horsing around the quarry, I began to change my mind. It was kind of neat the way he paid attention to Oliver, treating him like a little brother. He didn't leave Oliver out, the way most older kids would. And it seemed as if Lewis really cared about Mrs. Monicure. Of course, he was a big showoff and a total jerk sometimes. But maybe he acted that way to cover up the hurt he felt when his father didn't want him. That must have been a pretty big hurt.

And another thing, Lewis sure had a lot of imagination—not like me. He could come up with the wackiest ideas, but they were fun. Life at Mrs. M.'s sure had not been dull since Lewis came.

"Sandra!" Oliver shouted. "Come look what Lewis found!"

I glanced up. Lewis was on the other side of the quarry. A huge oak tree leaned over the open pit. A rope dangled from one high branch.

"Kids must have put this here," Lewis called. His voice bounced off the quarry walls. "I bet they used to swing over the water and jump in."

"Lewis," I said anxiously, walking toward the

tree. "Come on. Let's go! Mrs. M. will miss us."

"Wait a minute," he said. "I want to see if I can climb this tree." He shinnied partly up the trunk, and reached for the rope. "Cinchy. I bet I could swing over the pool," he bragged. "Like Tarzan."

"Lewis!" I screamed, panic filling my throat. "Get down from there!"

"You think I'm chicken? I'm not a scaredy-cat like you, Sandra." He got a grip on the rope with one hand and gave it a tug, testing its strength. "Watch this, you guys!"

"Lewis!" My scream echoed around the quarry.

Lewis closed both hands around the rope and pushed off from the tree trunk. He seemed to hang in midair for a split second, and then the rope tightened as he swung out. "Ah-ah-ah-ah-ah!" he screamed, imitating Tarzan.

His feet skimmed the scummy surface of the pool, and then pointed skyward. I could see his shoes scrabbling for a rocky foothold on the rim of the quarry.

The rope snapped, and Lewis fell backward.

This time his scream was real.

Eight

LEWIS seemed to fall in slow motion. His arms flew up, and he toppled back, back, back. My shoes seemed nailed to the ground. I couldn't have moved if someone had lit a stick of dynamite under me. I couldn't even scream.

Oliver moved first. He ran along the rim of the quarry to where Lewis disappeared and looked down. I saw him kneel and reach down with one hand. He yelled back over his shoulder, "Sandra! Get over here!"

My feet came unnailed then. I stumbled down the hill, half sliding on the seat of my jeans, tripping over brambles and bushes. By the time I got to Oliver, his face was red from the effort of hanging on to Lewis.

Lewis had only fallen about four or five feet. He clung desperately to a skinny, little sapling growing out of the side of the quarry wall. His foothold was shaky. I could see that if the sapling broke, he would drop into the pool. And there was no way out but up, straight up the cliff walls.

Even though Oliver gripped Lewis's wrist with all his might, he wasn't very strong. He wouldn't be able to stop Lewis from falling if the spindly tree snapped.

"Lewis," I cried, "are you okay?"

"Do I *look* like I'm okay?" Even hanging on for dear life, Lewis had a smart remark.

"We can't pull him up," I said to Oliver. "He's too heavy."

"Thanks," Lewis said.

"No offense," I said. "But you are."

"I guess it's all those snacks Mrs. M. feeds us." Lewis managed a sickly smile. "But I'm kind of tired of hanging on here. I mean, can't you guys *do* something?"

I thought fast.

"Oliver, go back to Mrs. M.'s. She'll get help.

113

I'll stay here with Lewis." When Oliver hesitated, I said, "Hurry! Run!"

I kneeled on the rock ledge and clasped Lewis's wrist just below Oliver's hand. Oliver pulled himself up and took off. He dashed up the hillside in record time, and then disappeared.

Shifting my knees on the rocky ledge, I settled in for a long stay. My hand was already becoming sweaty. No matter what, I couldn't let go.

He looked up at me. His face was pale—every freckle stood out as if it'd been drawn on with a marker. His gray eyes were wide with fear.

"You won't let go of me, will you? If I fall, I-I can't swim, Sandra. I can't even float."

"I won't let go. I promise." Then I asked, "Does your arm hurt? Where I'm pulling it?"

"Some. What's killing me is my leg. A pointy rock is sticking in me, and I can't move away from it." After a bit, he said, "I guess that was dumb, swinging on a rotten rope."

"It was pretty stupid," I said. "But I'll say this for you, you've got lots of nerve."

He grinned. "Lots of guts, too, huh?"

"*Too* much guts."

"Sandra, could you scratch my nose? It itches right on top. Right there."

Right then I realized that Lewis Butler would never change. He'd always be a pest. But I guess I had to admit, I sort of liked him.

He blabbed away. I could tell he was trying to take his mind off his sore arm and the fact he was dangling over a bottomless pool. "At least I gave you something to write about," he said. "You can write about the Great Quarry Rescue for your write-a-book project."

"Except you haven't been rescued yet," I reminded him. "I have to know how it turns out before I can write it."

"I hope your story has a happy ending," he said. His words were brave, but his shaky voice sounded scared, really scared.

My father once told me that fear was catching, like the flu. If Lewis knew I was scared spitless, he'd become even more scared and maybe fall. I tried to act like the whole thing was no big deal. Pretending to be bored, I said, "Oh, I don't think

116

this is exciting enough for a whole book. I have to have more stuff to write about."

"Put in the witch business," Lewis suggested, adjusting his position. His legs and arms were probably cramping something awful. "*That* ought to fill up a book!"

Just then his foot slipped. Lewis cried out. My hand nearly slid off his wrist, but I caught him in time. He tipped his head back to look at me.

"It's okay," he said. "I think..."

"Are you scared?" I asked.

"Uh, no," he replied, but I knew better.

"Mrs. M. will bring help," I reassured him. "She ought to be here soon. While we're waiting you can...tell me what you want for Christmas."

"What I want *right now* is to get out of here." Then he said something that about surprised my socks off. "Sandra, I want you to know something. I think—well, you're okay. For a girl."

My answer just sort of blurted out before I could think about what I was saying. "I guess you're okay, too," I said. "For a boy."

"You really aren't a scaredy-cat," he went on.

117

"I just said that stuff to rag you."

Whew, I thought, *Lewis must be desperate.*

"I hope our folks don't take us away from Mrs. M.'s," he said. "I'd like to stay. It's fun there."

Yeah, especially since you came, I almost said. But I choked back the words. Lewis would probably be rescued. No sense getting all gooey.

My own fingers were aching from clutching his wrist so tightly. "I'll never write again," I joked. "Or play the violin."

"The world thanks you," came his faint reply. He hung his head down instead of looking up at me. I could tell he was growing more tired by the second. I wasn't sure how much longer I could hang on myself.

Minutes, which seemed like hours, passed in tense silence. Lewis slid slowly down the cliff. The sapling was bent double under his weight. I had to lean farther and farther over the ledge to keep my grip. If help didn't come soon...

"Where are they?" I muttered.

"Do you think Mrs. M. will bring her witch friends?" Lewis asked.

"I don't care if she brings Dracula and Frankenstein." I wiped sweat off my upper lip with my free hand. "Just so *somebody* comes."

A few more minutes crawled by. Then Lewis said in a voice so faint that I could hardly hear him, "Sandra, I did something terrible."

"So what's new, Lewis?" I said. "You're *always* doing something terrible."

"This is different." He shifted his feet, knocking loose a shower of pebbles that dropped one by one into the pool. The pebbles sank without a trace. "I wrote a letter to my dad. It was real mean. I told him I hated him and I didn't ever want to see him again. Because he didn't want to keep me the last two months of school. And I mailed it."

I felt sorry for poor Lewis. It was bad enough his life hung in the balance without him feeling guilty, too.

"It's okay," I said. "When you get out of here, you can call him and tell him you didn't mean it. He'll understand."

"I don't know if he will."

119

"No, really. Parents understand more than you think." I thought about my own folks. Except for riding me about school all the time, my parents were pretty decent. They were forever telling me that they only wanted the best for me. When I tried to imagine what it would be like to not have one of them around, I decided maybe they were right about school, too.

"Lewis," I said suddenly, "I figured out a way we can stay at Mrs. M.'s."

"How?"

"We'll give our folks what they want, if they let us stay. I'll do better in school, and you can make up with your dad, and Oliver can quit fighting with his mother."

Lewis shook his head. "No. We can't bribe our parents to let us stay at Mrs. M.'s. We have to show that we're responsible for our own actions. That's what my mom tells me whenever I want to do something. It won't work. Not after today."

His feet stumbled again. The sapling snapped under the pressure. Lewis swung out over the pool. Suddenly the only thing keeping him from

120

tumbling into the water below was me. He tilted his head. On his face was a look of pure terror.

"Sandra! I can't..." he whispered, and I felt him slip away.

I threw myself flat on the ledge and leaned way over to grab him with my other hand. I knew I couldn't pull Lewis to safety—he was too heavy. But maybe I could buy a few more seconds.

Just when I thought I couldn't hold on any longer, we heard thrashing sounds in the woods above the quarry. Oliver crashed through the brush, followed by Mrs. Monicure.

"They're here!" I cried. "The tree broke! Hurry!"

"I'm coming," Mrs. M. shouted.

For an older lady, Mrs. Monicure came down that hill like a bullet. She climbed up on the ledge and rushed over to me. I noticed she had on her feather necklace.

"Lewis, for heaven's sake!" she said calmly. "Hang on, dear heart. We'll have you out of there in a jiffy."

My own heart sank. I thought she'd bring back help, the next door neighbor or somebody.

I knew there was no way the two of us could pull Lewis out. He weighed a ton.

She knelt down and replaced one of my hands with her own grip. "On the count of three, we'll yank, okay?" she said to me. "But first..."

With her other hand, she held the feather necklace out, as if she were offering it to the sky. She mumbled some strange words I didn't understand. Then she grabbed Lewis's arm just above my grip with both hands.

"Ready, Sandra?" she asked. "One, two, three!"

I closed my eyes and we pulled. Lewis flew up as if he were made out of feathers himself. He lay gasping on the ledge without speaking.

I flexed my fingers, trying to get a little blood back into them. "Boy!" I said. "We don't know our own strength, do we, Mrs. M.?"

"You just have to have faith," she said, stroking Lewis's hair. "Are you all right, dear?"

He rolled over. "Yeah, I guess so. Thanks."

"You had me worried sick," Mrs. Monicure said. "When Oliver told me where you were and what happened, I couldn't bear it that one of my kids was in trouble."

Lewis massaged his arm, glancing over at me with a little smile. I could tell he liked being one of Mrs. M.'s kids. We all did, for that matter.

Mrs. Monicure helped him stand up. She led him out of the clearing and up the wooded hillside. Oliver and I trailed behind.

"It's the strangest thing," I whispered to Oliver. "Lewis weighed as much as a hippo, but we pulled him up as if he were lighter than air!"

"It was the necklace," Oliver said.

"What do you mean?"

"The necklace Mrs. M. has on. It's called a witch's ladder. Nine feathers tied on a cord. Witches use them to make their spells stronger." He polished his glasses on the hem of his shirt. "I read about it in that book."

I gawked at him. "You mean...she used magic?" Then I remembered the weird words that Mrs. M. mumbled over the necklace. My jaw dropped. "She used magic!" I whispered.

Oliver held my arm, and we stopped walking. He said in a little voice, "Mrs. M. told me not to tell, but I know it's all right to tell you, Sandra."

"What, Oliver?"

"On the way over here," Oliver explained, "she said, 'I hope I have enough power left to help the boy.' I asked her what she meant, and she just smiled and said, 'You'll see, Oliver.'"

I gasped. "You mean, she told you that she was a witch?"

"Well, not exactly," Oliver said. "But I had the feeling that *she* knew that *we* knew. And it worked. She *did* have enough power to help us."

* * * * *

Mrs. Monicure didn't use magic to make us all a cup of hot chocolate. But it tasted delicious. And so did the extra-thick peanut butter and banana sandwiches she made us. Lewis ate two sandwiches, and he didn't even like peanut butter.

"Now. Suppose you tell me why you went to the quarry," Mrs. M. asked us.

I dunked my marshmallow in my hot chocolate, avoiding her eyes.

"It was me," Lewis spoke up. "I found an old map with the quarry on it. I talked the others into going with me. It's all my fault. Really!"

I couldn't let Lewis take all the blame. "It wasn't all Lewis's fault, Mrs. M.," I said. "I went because...because I thought we'd get in trouble, and Lewis would get blamed and—"

"Go on," she prompted.

I took a deep breath. "And you would send him away. Then it would be like before—me and you and Oliver."

Lewis stared at me. "You want to get rid of me?" Before, he would have looked mad. But now he looked as if he was going to cry.

"I-I was jealous because Oliver liked you better than me."

"But I like you both the same," Oliver said.

"But you wanted to get rid of me," Lewis repeated in a choking voice. "Why?"

I searched my brain for some kind of an excuse and realized I had to cough up the truth. "When you first came here, you were a real pest," I said to him. "You punched me and made fun of

Oliver. I mean, who could like you?"

Mrs. M. squeezed his shoulder. "It's hard, moving to a new town, leaving behind your friends."

"You've got new friends now," Oliver said.

"Two of the best friends any person could want," I said. "What more can you ask for?"

"Maybe some more hot chocolate," Lewis said, holding out his mug for Mrs. M. to refill. "And to stay here forever."

She brought the pan over to the table and filled Lewis's mug. "Hot chocolate I can arrange. Staying here, I don't know about."

"Why not?" I asked. "We want to stay. All of us. We like it here."

Mrs. M. sighed. "I wish it were that easy. I have to tell your parents about today. I couldn't keep it from them."

"No, you're right," I said glumly. "But none of it is your fault."

She smiled. "This is a matter for your parents to handle." She gathered empty plates and cups and carried them into the kitchen.

Oliver touched my arm. "It'll be okay, won't it, Sandra?" I knew he couldn't bear to lose another person he was close to.

"I hope you're right, Oliver, and that Mrs. M. does have enough power to help us," I said with my chin on my hand. "We need magic in the worst way. Or else we're sunk."

Nine

IT was almost as if we had used witchcraft ourselves at the meeting our parents had. But I'm getting ahead of myself again.

Of course, when Mrs. Monicure told our parents what had happened at the quarry, they practically went off the chart. My mother insisted that they all get together and discuss the matter.

The meeting was held at our house the very next night. We all sat in our living room. Oliver, Lewis, and I kept sneaking glances at each other. We were really nervous.

The grownups had coffee first, while they chit-chatted about the weather and the cost of houses. Then my mother brought up the reason that they were meeting.

"Well, we've heard from Mrs. Monicure," she said, setting her cup in the saucer with a clink. "Now let's hear the story from you children."

We had decided earlier that Lewis would be our spokesperson. He could talk a blue streak, for one thing, and grownups listened to him. We had also decided to tell the truth and shoulder the blame completely, all of us. It was the only way to get Mrs. Monicure off the hook.

"I found a map," Lewis began, "that one the real estate lady gave us when we first moved here. Anyway, the map showed this old quarry. I thought it would be neat to go and find it. It didn't look very far from Mrs. M.'s. So I asked Sandra and Oliver if they wanted to go, and they both said yes."

"You left Mrs. Monicure's property even though you have been told time and again not to?" my father asked.

"Yes," Lewis answered. "We knew we were doing wrong, but we didn't think it would hurt anything. We planned to go find the quarry and be back before anyone missed us. It didn't quite work out that way," he added.

"Lewis, you could have been killed," Mrs. Butler said. She was a plump woman with sandy hair and faded freckles. Lewis looked just like her. "You could have drowned! He can't swim a lick," she told the other parents.

"But I *didn't,*" he argued. "Sandra and Oliver and Mrs. Monicure saved me. We promise we won't do it again. Don't we, guys?" Oliver and I murmured that we wouldn't ever go near the old quarry again.

"And we won't leave Mrs. M.'s property, either," I said. "Not unless she's with us."

Then Oliver said what we all felt. "We want to stay at Mrs. Monicure's. You shouldn't blame her for what we did."

At that point, Oliver's mother put her coffee cup on the table. She was the opposite of Oliver. Instead of blond hair and blue eyes, Mrs. Cantrell had short dark hair and big brown eyes. There were lines around her eyes that I don't remember being there when Oliver's father was alive.

"Kids, I think your parents and I would like to

continue this discussion in private. Would you mind going into another room?" she said.

My mother ushered us out of the living room. She said, "Sandra, take Lewis and Oliver into the den. Watch TV or play a video game, okay?"

As soon as she went back into the living room, Lewis whipped around and asked, "Where can we listen from?"

I know it was wrong to eavesdrop, but our whole future with Mrs. Monicure was at stake.

"The kitchen," I said. "We can hide behind the counter."

We turned on the television so that our parents would think we were watching it, and then sneaked into the kitchen. The kitchen was divided from the dining room by a counter. The living room was right next to the dining room. We couldn't see, but we could hear them talking.

"—think they're testing the waters." That was my mother. "They've had a lot of adjustments to make lately, especially Oliver. This is just their way of striking out."

"And getting back," Mrs. Butler said, somewhat unhappily. "Lewis has been so miserable since the move. He had to leave Olney almost at the end of the school year, his friends...I begged his father to take him until summer, but..."

Lewis made a face.

"Oliver has been a handful lately, too," Mrs. Cantrell said. "He really resents my dating."

My father spoke next. "Sandra gets more notes from school than any kid I've ever known."

It was my turn to make a face. This was the way our parents talked about us when we weren't around. Or when they *thought* we weren't around!

"In addition to their regular problems, they've had to adjust to each other," my mother said. "Since they're very different children, I'm sure it's been difficult."

"But they seem to get along fine now," Mrs. Cantrell said. "In fact, Oliver talks about Lewis and Sandra day and night. They're like another family to him."

Oliver studied his tennis shoes with an embarrassed grin on his face.

"—exactly," my mother was saying. "They

support one another. And I believe those children have benefited from being together at Mrs. Monicure's. She is a wonderful sitter."

Mrs. Cantrell's voice dropped. "What about this witch business?"

"It's another way of striking out," my mother replied. "Didn't you say you were out on a date when Oliver left the house that night? Of course he wants you to worry! You two have been so close since your husband's death. Now he's afraid you might replace his affection with someone else's."

Lewis rolled his eyes at me. This was heavy stuff. When were they going to get to the part where they would decide about Mrs. Monicure?

"—does seem to be a capable lady," Lewis's mother said. "I liked her the minute I met her. Except for what happened today, I'd say that Lewis has settled down quite a bit since he's been going to her house after school. I give a lot of credit to Mrs. Monicure."

Lewis crossed his fingers. I did too. Oliver crossed his fingers on both hands. Wasn't crossing your fingers a kind of magic?

"Sandra hasn't brought a note home in at least two weeks," my father said. "I think the children are a good influence on each other. It would be a shame to split them up."

"Or take them away from Mrs. Monicure's," said my mother.

Way to go, Mom! I cheered silently. She was in our corner all along!

"They do like it there," Mom added.

"But what about today?" Mrs. Butler said with concern. "They ran off and got in trouble!"

"I have a feeling it won't happen again," my dad said. "We were talking about getting them a new sitter, remember? They probably felt threatened, and so they took action. It was a way to get our attention."

"I say we let them stay at Mrs. Monicure's," my mother said. "As Jack said, they really seem to be good for each other."

"I do need someone to watch Lewis all day this summer while I'm at work," Mrs. Butler said. "I'm willing, if Mrs. Monicure is." She chuckled. "Poor woman. I wonder if she knows what she is letting herself in for—Lewis for a whole day!"

I muffled a giggle. Lewis did not look amused.

"If you three feel that strongly..." said Mrs. Cantrell. "I guess Oliver would be heartbroken if I moved him to a new sitter. His heart has been broken enough lately..."

Before Oliver could get that sad expression on his face, I reached over and shook his hand. Lewis shook mine, and then Oliver's.

We did it.

My father was laughing. "Those kids! Thinking Mrs. Monicure is a witch! I mean, can you imagine anyone less witchy than her?"

They all laughed at the crazy idea of Mrs. M. being a witch. Lewis, Oliver, and I just smiled.

* * * * *

In the trees overhead, birds sang and squabbled, making so much racket that I could hardly concentrate on what I was writing. Bees hummed in the rose bushes. I could sit in the wooden swing Mrs. Monicure had painted pink and sniff the roses all day. But I had to finish my project.

Oliver gently prodded a ladybug into his new bug cage. It had wire screen all the way around and was much kinder to the insects than stuffing them in an old jar with holes punched in the lid.

He squinted at me in the June sunlight. "Aren't you done yet?"

"Almost," I said, scribbling on my clipboard. I wrote a few more words, and then leaned back against the pink and blue cushion.

I love June. It's my favorite month of the year. It used to be my favorite because that's the month school is out for the summer. Now it's my favorite because it's so nice in Mrs. Monicure's garden.

Lewis came outside, carefully balancing three glasses of grapeade. He clenched a big bag of pretzels in his teeth.

"'ake 'is," he told Oliver, meaning the bag of pretzels.

Oliver took the pretzels and opened the bag.

136

Lewis handed me my drink.

"Thank you," I said. I felt like a princess among the flowers with people bringing me food.

"Guess what." Lewis said. "I can't find the weathermaking spell."

"What do you want that for?" I asked suspiciously. We had promised our folks we would behave at Mrs. Monicure's. No funny business, like cooking up a storm. Besides, we didn't need magic any more. We had Lewis who was always full of ideas.

Lewis grinned. "I thought a little thunderstorm would be neat. It's kind of dry here."

"Lewis..." I warned.

"Don't worry," he answered. "I couldn't find it anyway. It wasn't in the flower pot. She must have moved it." Lewis took a big drink, giving himself a grape mustache.

Sitting in the warm sunlight with my two friends, I thought about Mrs. M. She had never mentioned magic again after that time she told Oliver she hoped she had enough power to help us. But the funny thing was, she hadn't needed to talk about it. We knew she had her power back, and I'm pretty sure that she knew that *we* knew—just like Oliver said.

Ever since she had rescued Lewis, Mrs. M. had seemed a lot happier. She walked around singing and laughing. Of course, maybe she was glad our parents didn't take us away. Or maybe it was something else.

I remember the day after she went to the May witches' meeting. She seemed happy as a lark. We kids knew it must have been that she was back as a full member. Her spells were working again. But we never said anything about magic to Mrs. M.

That is, not until now.

"I'm going to ask her," Lewis announced suddenly.

"You can't!" I cried, shocked.

"Don't worry," he said. "I'll ask her so that she won't be suspicious."

Sure you will, I thought.

Mrs. Monicure came out just then, and I shot Lewis a dirty look. She sat with her own glass of grapeade. Mrs. M. wasn't like most grownups—she ate and drank what we kids did.

"Beautiful day," she said, sitting next to me on the swing. She wore a loose pink dress and pink sandals with plastic daisies on the straps. I crammed my clipboard behind a cushion. I didn't want her to see what I was writing.

"Almost like a magic day," Lewis said. I rolled my eyes. "Do you believe in magic, Mrs. M.?" he asked.

"Yes, I do believe in magic, Lewis," she answered with a twinkle in her eye. "Some things are so special that they must have a sprinkle of magic in them. Like friendship, for instance. Take you kids. In the beginning, you didn't get along at all. But now you're best of friends. If that's not magic, I don't know what is."

"Ah, I don't mean that kind," Lewis said. "I mean real magic, like the kind witches do."

Mrs. M. just smiled and rocked the swing. "Friendship *is* real magic, Lewis," she said.

Leave it to Lewis to not know when to stop. "Mrs. M.," he asked, "if you were a witch, what kind of witch would you be?"

I held my breath. Oliver stopped chewing his pretzel.

Mrs. M. laughed, pushing the swing with the toe of one sandaled foot. "What kind of witch do *you* think I'd be?"

"An ordinary one," said Lewis.

"An everyday witch," I added.

"A good witch, definitely," Oliver said.

"Then that's the kind I'd be," Mrs. M. said. "*If* I were a witch. Now I think I'd better go put a spell on my tomato plants, if I want any tomatoes this summer." She got up and went over to the vegetable section of her garden.

I just shook my head at Lewis. He could be impossible sometimes. But I'd learned to like him. I had even started to try to be more like him—in one way at least. I tried to use my imagination more, to try to have more fun.

As we drank our drinks, the three of us watched Mrs. M. putter among her tomato plants. She had mislaid her garden trowel and was searching for it.

SNAP

"Trowel," we heard her say. She snapped her fingers.

Then suddenly, just as with the salt shaker, the trowel was right by her foot. Had it been there all along? Or had she made it appear?

I knew what Lewis thought because he whispered right away, "Now *that's* what I call magic!"

"That might be magic," I answered, "but Mrs. M. is right. Friendship is real magic, too."

A—

Terrific story, Cassandra! The best write-a-book project I've ever read. It's so well-written, I almost think it really happened! You would have gotten an A plus, if you hadn't turned it in late. Keep up the good work!

Mr. Crowley

About the Author

Candice F. Ransom never had a witch for a babysitter (though she sometimes wondered about her sister). The origin of this book goes back to her childhood, when she and her cousins would huddle behind the furnace in a pitch-dark basement and tell stories to scare each other.

The author of over 30 books, both scary and regular, Candice Ransom lives in Centreville, Virginia with her husband and her black cat. She's always on the lookout for a little magic, but the cat is bone-lazy and her electric broom doesn't do anything unless it's plugged in.

Among her books for Willowisp Press are *Today Fifth Grade, Tomorrow the World, The Funniest Sixth-Grade Video Ever!*, and *The Love Charm.*